MW01068921

Boystown

Three Nick Nowak Mysteries

Marshall Thornton

Los Angeles
2015

Copyright © 2009, 2011, 2015 Marshall Thornton

This book is a work of fiction. Names, characters, places, and incidents are products of the author's imagination or are used fictitiously. Any resemblance to actual events or locales or persons, living or dead, is entirely coincidental.

This book is licensed to the original purchaser only. Duplication or distribution via any means is illegal and a violation of International Copyright Law, subject to criminal prosecution and upon conviction, fines and/or imprisonment.

All rights reserved, including the right of reproduction in whole or in part in any form.

Published by Kenmore Books
Edited by Vincent Diamond
Additional Editing by Joan Martinelli
Cover design by Marshall Thornton
Image by Stefanie Mohr 123RF Stock Photos

ISBN-13: 978-1507835296
ISBN-10: 1507835299

Second Edition

While I actually lived in Chicago during the early eighties, memory plays tricks on all of us and more research was necessary than I'd expected when I began the *Boystown Mysteries*. The Internet is, of course, an amazing resource and I have consulted many historical sites. I would like to single out Sukie de La Croix who's written about gay Chicago history for several publications and Chicago Gay History whose website features remarkable videos of gay Chicagoans.

I would also like to thank my readers, editors, and memory checkers: Danielle Wolff, Miles Ketchum, Joan Martinelli, Ellen Sue Feinberg, Robin Sinclair, and Vincent Diamond.

Little Boy Found

Like most guys, I'm a sucker for easy sex and a fast buck. Unlike most guys, I should know better.

The call came in a few minutes after three on a Tuesday afternoon. I rent a small office in a soon-to-be-demolished granite and marble building located at the south end of the Loop. There's just room enough for a desk, a metal file cabinet, a chair for a client, and a dead corn plant I keep meaning to throw out. That particular day there wasn't anything on the radio except reporters droning on about the inauguration. It seemed a little odd that none of them complained that our country was now going to be run by a guy who once co-starred with a chimp. Not that I had anything against the Gipper. I just wasn't convinced I wanted his finger on the button. I turned the radio down and picked up the phone.

"Is this Nick Nowak?" the voice on the other end asked. It was some guy, trying not to sound as nervous as he obviously was.

"Sure is," I replied. I reached into my desk to pull out my cigarettes. Then I remembered I'd quit at New Year's. A decision I'd regretted every day since.

"The private investigator?" the guy asked.

"Yeah, the private investigator." I wondered how many other varieties of Nick Nowak he thought were out there. "What can I do for you?"

The line crackled for a beat. Then he said, "I need you to find someone for me."

I looked out my eighth story window, watched as a couple flakes of snow drifted down to LaSalle Street, and waited for the guy to tell me who it was he wanted me to find. He didn't. Great. This was gonna be like pulling teeth.

"Let's start with you," I said. "What's your name?"

"Walt...Paddington. Walt Paddington."

"Well, Walt, why don't you come down to my office and we'll talk about this person you want me to find."

"I can't do that."

"What? You're the shy type?"

"I'm downstate. Carbondale." At least it was a logical excuse. Carbondale is at one end of the state, Chicago at the other. It's quite a hike.

"Who do you want me to find?"

"My...my friend."

I waited. I was beginning to feel like the dentist who kept an office down the hall. "Come on, Walt, you're gonna need to be a little more specific."

"His name is Brian Peerson. He's just twenty-one. Very sweet. He's been gone almost a year."

"And you just now decided to look for him?"

"I thought I'd stop missing him, but I didn't." There was real shame in his voice, though for what I couldn't be sure. "I just need to find him. The sooner the better."

The situation was getting clearer. Walt sounded older; maybe he was, maybe he wasn't, but he sounded it. And it made sense; an older, small-town guy wants to find his twinkie boyfriend who's run off to the big city. Willing to pay a private investigator to do it. Yeah, I got the picture. There was just one problem.

"Why me?" I asked.

"What?" I could almost hear him jump.

"I said 'why me.' How'd you come to find me?"

"Yellow Pages."

"I don't think so." I had an ad in the Yellow Pages, all right. It said "Nick Nowak, Private Investigator." It gave my license number and listed a couple of things I specialize in. Background checks. Security. Skip trace. What it didn't say was, "Big Old Fag ready to find your missing boyfriend." It was no coincidence Paddington had called me.

I waited. Finally he said, "You were recommended."

"By?"

"I'd rather not say."

I didn't like it. Didn't like it at all. Part of me wanted to give him the brush off, but business had been slow since the holidays. I told him to send some pictures of the kid, a written physical description, former addresses, social security number if he had it, an explanation of why he thought the kid was in Chicago, anything else he thought might help, and exactly double my normal retainer.

I figured I'd never hear from the guy again.

# # #

In another life I was a cop. Born and bred. Grew up in Bridgeport on the south side. I've got a father and two brothers on the job, three uncles, five cousins, and a couple of aunts doing clerical in Records. Most of them are named Nowak, but there are a few Latowskis and Dudas thrown in. None of them talk to me. Not since an unfortunate incident resulted in my abrupt departure from the department.

The rest of that week I spent doing background checks for Peterson-Palmer Investments, a brokerage firm that throws work my way. They like anyone with access to actual cash accounts to be felony-free, living under their right name, and not a drunk, a druggie, or an inveterate gambler. It can be tedious work, but it keeps a roof over my head. Well, part of the roof, anyway.

It took some doing, but I found a decent jazz station on the radio. This was a relief since all the other stations were now blathering about the hostages being released. For some reason they all kept giving the credit to the Gipper, even though he hadn't even been president an hour when it happened. To me, it seemed more like the camel jockeys just wanted to stick it to the peanut farmer and it didn't have a whole lot to do with the skill of the incoming commander in chief.

That Thursday I popped down to Oak Street on the way home from my office. Hunched between the elegant boutiques is a bar called The Loading Zone where they run a well-attended happy hour every afternoon. Below street level, the place was smoky and already crowded when I walked in.

I wore a thin wool overcoat that was too light for a Chicago winter, so I compensated with a corduroy blazer and flannel shirt underneath. The outfit was a little formal for a gay bar, but it allowed my holster and the 9mm Sig Sauer it held to go unnoticed. Some people might not find it necessary to walk around with a gun tucked under their arm. They're lucky.

I checked the overcoat and wandered over to the bar to order a Miller and a shot of tequila. I'm six foot three, weigh a steady two-ten, and in a personal ad I might have the nerve to put VGL—after about three beers. I'm thirty-two, and I still get my fair share of attention at places like The Loading Zone. I visit the Y a couple times a week, but I'm not what you'd call muscular, just fit. My dark hair gets curly if I let it grow too long, so I keep it short. My mustache makes me look a little like a clone, but the fact that my 501s aren't two sizes too small takes me out of the running.

I downed the shot and was halfway through my beer when I noticed a kid in the crowd staring at me. I stared back. He was short and thick, the kind of guy who would have made a good wrestler in high school—if he wasn't so busy flitting around the drama club. His hair was sand-colored and flopped lazily over one blue eye. He wore a tight thermal undershirt that had been dyed a bright turquoise. His designer jeans had been mercilessly tailored to show off his thick thighs and his perky, round ass. When I walked over, his name turned out to be Bobby. Bobby Something-or-Other. The bar was loud, and I didn't exactly pick up his last name. Not that I cared.

As he flamboyantly smoked one extra long cigarette after another, Bobby told me he worked at the Chicago Apparel Center in a showroom for ladies' accessories: scarves, belts, and handbags. He was devoted to Jane Olivor, Barbara Cook, and Bette Midler. He'd studied theater in college and heard that Chicago was a great theater town, but no one would give him a break. I guess there weren't a lot of parts for guys who smoked like Bette Davis. Mostly, I just watched that cigarette, debating whether to bum one.

On Saturdays, he took an acting class that cost him a small fortune. A New York director would put the half dozen budding actors on stage and tell them to do whatever they liked as long as they 'inhabited' the space. Then he'd make sarcastic comments about what the actors had done until they were quivering emotional wrecks.

He accused Bobby of masturbating on stage.

"Were you?" I asked.

"He probably would have liked that." Bobby laughed and added, "Maybe I'll try it next week."

He launched into a discussion of his favorite actresses, most of whom were dead or close to it. Also a writer he adored and I'd never heard of, James Kirkwood. And, when his drink was empty, how much he liked Long Island Iced Teas. I bought him one, and later another.

Finally, after he'd given me far more information about himself than I actually wanted, he agreed to go home with me. When we got outside the bar, the temperature had dropped a good twenty degrees and hovered just above life threatening. There was no way I was going to stand at a bus station or drag my ass over to the El, so I hailed us a cab.

It was a Checker. I like Checker cabs. They feel like the real thing. The Chevy Impalas and Ford LTDs floating around the city didn't do it for me. I told the driver to head up to my apartment on Roscoe near Halsted. On the way, Bobby told me the most intimate secrets of his three roommates. In the more than two hours I'd been with him, he'd asked me only three questions. What was my name? What did I do for a living? And was I a top? So far this was my favorite thing about Bobby. Well, if you didn't count the fact that he slipped his hand into my lap as the driver pulled out onto Lake Shore Drive.

My apartment is what's called a garden apartment, which is what landlords name a basement after they fix it up and put it up for rent. The windows sit level with the sidewalk, and I get a good view of people from the waist down. From the layout, it's clear it wasn't supposed to be an apartment at all. You walk into the building's foyer and next to the mailboxes is my front door. Once you open that, you're in a ten or twelve-foot hallway, then down a couple of steps into a funky little room that is six feet by six feet. It would have made a nice little reading area with a chair and lamp, I suppose. But I'm not inclined that way.

From there you go into a normal-sized room with a window, but no closet and no actual door. It's a junk room. There are a couple boxes full of stuff I don't want to look at; a box full of high school memorabilia, pay stubs from every job I ever had, all my check registers, a bike with a flat tire I never got fixed. Bobby gave the room a sniff and then charged on to the rest of the apartment.

Next comes the living room, a bathroom, my bedroom, and the rarely used kitchen. The place is laid out like a conch shell wrapping in on itself: from the burglar-barred window in the funky little not-a-reading room, you practically stare into the barred kitchen window. Along the ceiling snakes an assortment of pipes and radiators.

Bobby nosed around trying to make sense of the place. Actually, it was nicely decorated. Soft gray walls, bright white molding, refinished floors, custom mini-blinds. I take no responsibility for any of that. I helped sand the floors and did a little painting, but none of it was my idea. I don't have that kind of vision.

What furniture I still have is sitting exactly where it started out. So there are some holes where pieces have been subtracted. For instance, there are two nice director's chairs in the living room facing a big empty spot where a sofa ought to be. My albums and a pretty decent component stereo sit on the floor where a set of shelves once held them.

Bobby eyed the holes. "You should get some more furniture."

"I don't spend a lot of time sitting around," I replied. Then got down to business. "The bedroom's this way."

The bedroom, which was painted a soft blue, had little more than a mattress and a scarred three-drawer dresser. Without any prelude we began to take our clothes off, more like athletes about to engage in a sporting event than lovers. Bobby carefully folded his clothes and set them in a pile. I took my gun out of its holster and put it on top of the dresser. Bobby looked at it a moment, then asked, "Are you going to shoot me?"

"Are you going to give me a reason to?"

He laughed. I think he was little turned on by the idea of a gun being in the room. Before I'd finished with my shirt, Bobby had managed to get the rest of his clothes off. Wearing just a pair of black bikinis, he walked over and dropped to his knees.

I leaned over and flipped off the light, leaving the room lit by a sliver of light coming in from the hallway. He unbuttoned my jeans for me and pulled them down around my thighs. He chuckled a little. "Boxers? My father wears boxers."

"I'm not your father," I said, and pushed his head into my crotch. My dick slipped easily through the opening of my boxers and into Bobby's waiting mouth. He wrapped his hand around the base so it wouldn't go too far down his throat. I put up with that for a few minutes, while he tongued and licked the shaft. He pursed his lips and nibbled at my cock head like it was a strawberry.

When I was ready for something more serious, I pulled his hand away. I pushed my cock deep into his mouth, and he pulled away. "It's a little big for me."

I almost made a crack about him biting off more than he could chew, but decided not to bother. He wrapped his hand around my cock and went back to nibbling. I looked down and could see his dick swelling inside his little black panties.

Enough was enough. I pulled him off me and stood him up. I yanked down his bikini briefs and pushed him onto the bed. His prick wasn't very long, but it was nice and thick. Not that it mattered much to me right then. I was interested in the other side. With one hand, I flipped him over. That's the thing about short guys; they're easy to move around.

Bobby's breath grew rougher. He knew what was coming. Watching me over his shoulder, his mouth was wet and glistening. His ass was big, or at least big for his frame; buttocks standing up, round and tensed. I opened the top drawer of the dresser and pulled out a jar of Vaseline. Crawling onto the bed, I lubed up Bobby's ass and my dick, aimed quickly, and was in him.

He gasped. Then held his breath, forcing himself to relax. I pounded into him, fast and deep. I should have been more careful—but then, given the way he was panting and moaning, maybe not. The sound of my thighs slapping against his butt bounced off the walls.

Even in the dark, his skin was so white it nearly glowed. He turned his head back to look at me, and I pushed his face into the pillow. While I fucked him, I watched his spine twist as he took my cock over and over.

"Oh, God, you're fucking me," he said into the pillow.

"Don't talk," I told him. Then I slapped his ass. Hard. He must have liked it, because his sphincter clamped down on my dick like he wasn't ever going to let go. I slapped him again, just to make him squeeze me.

Pushing his hips up into me, he slipped his hand underneath and started jacking off. I fucked him harder and faster. He gave out a long, continuous moan that bounced a little each time I thrust into him.

Then he was coming, his ass contracting with each ejaculation. I kept fucking him like I barely noticed. He tried to take it, but he was one of those guys who got all sensitive after they come. He was nearly shivering each time I thrust into him.

Eventually he said, "Would you mind stopping?" I did mind. But I stopped anyway. I pulled out and plunked down next to him on the bed. He reached for my dick like he was going to go to work on it.

"Don't do that," I told him.

I took my cock in hand and started to pump. Squeezing the shaft tight, I twisted my fist each time I came to the top to run the better part of my palm across the head. It only took a dozen solid poundings and I came. Thick wads of creamy jizz landed in the curly, brown hair between my pecs.

Afterward, Bobby Something-or-other hung around. He wasn't the cuddly type, which was good. But he also wasn't the type who leaves. I was too tired to deal with it, so I just went to sleep. In the morning, I realized Bobby looked just like someone I didn't want to be thinking about, so I threw him out. Daylight does that sometimes.

# # #

When I got to my office that Friday, the package was leaning up against the door. It was a big manila envelope, the ten-by-thirteen kind. I brought it in, set it on the desk, and stared at it for a minute or two before I opened it. The first things that fell out were five crisp one-hundred-dollar bills. My retainer. Well, double my retainer.

I stacked the bills neatly on my blotter, then turned my attention to the other inhabitants of the envelope: several sheets of onionskin typing paper and a couple photos. I started with the photos.

One was a high school graduation shot, presumably Brian Peerson. In the shot, he wore a white puka shell necklace, an over-bright Qiana knit shirt, a big toothy smile, a tan, and a mop of curly hair. He looked like some surfer kid out in California. In the second photo, Brian stood on the stoop of a white house with green shutters. A blanket of snow covered the parts of the front yard that could be seen. He wore a pair of jeans with the bottoms rolled up, a corduroy vest, and a skinny tie. The curly hair had been cut short, and he smiled at the camera in a way that said he liked whoever was taking the picture.

The typing paper was watermarked. The information on it was typed using what looked to be a fairly recent portable typewriter. The kind you can pick up at any Sears or Montgomery Wards. I glanced at the envelope and noted that it had been sent with a typed label and no return address. The whole package seemed impersonal, and that bugged me.

One of the onionskin sheets listed a social security number and an address: Dolan Hall, Illinois Wesleyan in Bloomington. That was odd. Walt had said he was in Carbondale. I double-checked the postmark. It was smudged and hard to read, but it looked like it said Carbondale. How did good old Walt end up with a boyfriend half a state away? Beneath the address was a physical description of Brian: 5' 7", 155lbs, blond, blue-eyed, two-inch scar on his right thumb.

The second sheet proved more informative, or at least seemed to be. It was poorly typed, even though the typist had liberally employed Wite-Out. It said:

> Brian always loved Chicago & talked aboit it often.
> One of his early memories is of going to Marshall

Fields and talk to Santa CLaus. He got everything he wanted that yr and Chicago became magical place. Over the years, he went there a lot, at first with family or on school trips, later with friends. He said Chicago was 'like Land of Ox for him, except he never wanted to click his heals & go home.'

He left me about a year ago. I have gone to Chicago trying to find him but havent had luck. Brian is very social. He loves a party. Maybe, he drinks too much. I don't like to criticixe. He prefers hard booze to beer or wine. He likes good restaurants, old movies, books and Broadway musicals. HE likes older men. While in college he took business, but he didn't Like it. He made his own spending money by working in a pizxa parlor. Please find Brian as quckly as you can. I want to kno he's OK.

The last sheet was nothing but the typewritten sentence: *"WIll call Monday 2pm to check on progress."* I would have preferred a phone number; I had a few things I'd like to check on myself.

I picked up Brian's high school photo again and, in a flash, realized Brian Peerson looked a lot like the guy I fucked the night before, Bobby Somebody-or-other. Wouldn't that have been a kick, I thought. They weren't the same person, of course. But it would have been a kick.

That afternoon, I did the basic stuff you do when a person's missing. I checked with the morgue to see if there were any John Does who fit Brian's description. There weren't. At least he's alive, I thought. But then corrected myself. All I'd learned was that his body hadn't gone unclaimed in Chicago. It could be unclaimed in a hell of a lot of other places.

I called information to see if Brian had a phone in his name. I know that seems ridiculously simple, but sometimes it's the simple stuff that pays off. Of course, he might not be using his real name, or he might not have listed the number. I came up blank, so for exercise I walked the eleven blocks to the county clerk's office and checked for marriages, death certificates, and property registration. Nothing turned up. But then, I hadn't expected it to. I caught the El home.

On Fridays and Saturdays, I have a part-time gig working security at a nightclub on Broadway called Paradise Isle. Even though some radio disc jockey declared disco dead by burning a bunch of records at Comiskey Park about two years back, you wouldn't know it at Paradise Isle. The DJ is Miss Minerva Jones, the only drag queen I ever met who didn't have some sort of joke name. I like that about her. You can only meet Anita Mann so many times before it gets old. When it comes to disco, Miss Minerva is a purist. She plays Thelma Houston, Sylvester, Chic, and Sister Sledge. Sure, she also plays The Bee Gees, The Village People, and Gloria Gaynor's "I Will Survive," but only if you tip her.

The club is forty percent dance floor and always full. The dance floor is made of thick Plexiglas and lit from beneath. The rest of the place holds a couple dozen tables, some booths against the wall, and a bar that runs the length of the club. The theme is tropical, and there are a couple of neon palm trees attached to the walls. The bartenders start the night in Hawaiian print shirts, but have lost them by the time I show up at nine. When I first started, the owner, Davey Edwards, tried to get me to wear a paper lei. I put my foot down.

From ten to two I stand at the door with a flashlight and check IDs. Wearing a paper lei, Davey takes the cover charge. I could do the whole thing myself, but I'd have a bit of trouble balancing the cash drawer if a fight broke out. And they do break out every so often. Fortunately, most queens have to warm up with a couple rounds of catty remarks, so I'm usually there before anyone throws a punch.

That Friday was busy but uneventful. Davey stops charging a cover at one, so I'm alone for the last hour. Mostly people are leaving by then, so I spend my time saying "good night" and telling people, especially the drunk ones, to "be careful." After my shift, I usually head over to the bar for a couple of free drinks. That night was no different.

Ross weaved his way over and asked what I wanted. Even though it was below zero outside, his well-defined, bare chest was slick with sweat.

Ross is a sexy mix of boy and man. He's got freckles across the bridge of his nose and a cowlick on the left side of his forehead. He's also got biceps hovering around sixteen inches and a wad in his pants that strains the zipper on his Calvin Klein jeans.

After he brought me a beer, Ross offered me a Camel Light. I turned him down. "Willpower," he said. "I hate that in a man."

I pulled out Brian Peerson's high school graduation photo and showed it to him. "You see this kid around? During the week maybe."

He took the photo out of my hand and held it under the bar to catch the light. Then he handed it back to me. "I've probably seen a hundred kids that look like this in the last week."

"I figured."

"Why not show it to Eugene, see what he thinks?" I looked down the bar to one of the regulars, a squat little man with a bad comb-over. He was in his mid-thirties, but he looked fifty. Ross continued, "He's big on twinkies. He can even tell them apart."

I sipped my beer. "They actually talk to him?"

"When he buys them drinks. Every couple weeks he gets one drunk enough to take home."

I finished my beer and walked down the bar. After I introduced myself and told Eugene what I wanted, I pulled out Brian Peerson's photo. Eugene studied it and said, "Yeah. He was in The Closet a week or so before Christmas. I bought him a drink. He said 'thank you,' but other than that he wasn't very friendly."

"I need to find him for a client. Do you remember anything else?"

He stared at me blankly for a moment, then he said, "Black pants, white shirt." Not getting it, I shrugged. Eugene smiled. "A waiter."

"Ah," I said, then thanked him and gave him my card.

Pleased with myself, I went back down the bar and asked Ross for another beer. I knew three things about Brian I hadn't known before. He was alive. He was definitely in Chicago. And he worked at a restaurant.

Unfortunately, there had to be five hundred restaurants on the north side. I realized I might need a few extra copies of his photo.

# # #

The next morning, I woke up in the midst of receiving one of the better blow jobs in recent memory. It was cold in my apartment—the landlord controlled the heat and liked to keep it five degrees below the legal minimum—so Ross was burrowed deep under the covers with my cock in his mouth.

I let him go at it for a while, then said fuck it and threw back the covers so I could get a good look at what he was doing. It was cold for a moment or two, but I forgot about that quickly. My boxers were down around my knees, and Ross' head bobbed up and down along my shaft.

There was nothing timid about the way Ross sucked a cock. He didn't hold the base of my dick with one hand. He didn't nibble at the tip. Without even a moment's hesitation, he bobbed his head all the way down until my pubic hair was tickling his nose. After he did that enough times, I started to moan.

Ross let my cock drop out of his mouth and smiled up at me. "Good morning," he said, then slipped my right testicle into his mouth. He rolled it around gently, let it drop out of his mouth. and switched to the left. With his fingers he rubbed the spot behind my balls. Anxiously, I reached down and started jerking myself. Ross reached up and brushed my hand away.

Then he was sucking on the end of my dick, letting it pop in and out of his mouth. He ran his tongue up and down my shaft before he went back to deep-throating me.

"Yeah, that's it. Suck my dick." I knew Ross liked it when I talked. "Take it. Take it all the way."

I grabbed him by the back of the head and tried to get my prick in even deeper. Ross had his hand wrapped tight around my balls. Pulling them, twisting gently. I was close. It wasn't going to take much more before I—

With a spasm that shook my whole body, I came in three heavy spurts deep in the back of Ross's throat.

Crawling up the bed, Ross tucked himself in next to me. I held on to him while he jacked himself off. It didn't take long. I think he was almost there when I came in his throat. Barely a minute later he was coming all over his belly.

I suppose I could have returned the favor and sucked him off. But, for one thing, I was not as good at it and it was embarrassing to risk comparison. For another, he was technically someone else's boyfriend. If he really wanted a blow job, he could go ask his boyfriend.

Well, maybe boyfriend's not such a good word. Earl Silver was in his mid-forties and locally famous as a social columnist for the *Daily Herald*. He spent weeknights with Ross in the city and weekends in Naperville with the wife and kids. I figured if Ross was dumb enough to get in a situation like that, he deserved to miss out on the occasional blow job.

I went into the bathroom and cleaned myself up. I wet a washrag and brought it back to Ross. It was not the first time I'd ended up in bed with him. Given his situation, he was frequently at loose ends on Fridays and Saturdays when I happened to also be at loose ends.

After he finished wiping off his abs, Ross said, "That kid in the picture you showed me, he's just your type."

"I don't have a type."

"Yeah, you do. I see the guys you look at. Small, blond, they don't have to be young, but it helps."

"So, what's this about?" I wagged a finger back and forth between us. "You're not my type."

"Which you kindly overlook because I'm a really nice guy and a great fuck," he said. I wasn't going to let him know it, but he wasn't far off.

"How's the boyfriend?" I asked to change the subject.

"Earl is writing a book about our lady mayor. He says it's going to be scandalous. I think he's making half of it up."

"Sounds like a great guy."

He shrugged and said, "I love him," as though that made up for everything.

When Ross left, it was nearly noon. I'd have to hurry if I wanted to get much done. I zipped out and found a place that would make twenty-five copies of Brian's graduation photo in an hour. I grabbed a gyros for breakfast, then trudged over to the El. It was freezing on the platform, but I ate my gyros, which was nice and hot. Finally, a train came, and I took it down to LaSalle. I don't normally go to my office on Saturday, but I was curious about something and wanted to check it out.

My building, which is pretty quiet to begin with, is a morgue on weekends. I unlocked my office and went directly to my filing cabinet. I pulled out all my case files for the last year and a half. Actually, they were all my cases files, since that's how long I'd been on my own. I made a list of my clients and then sat staring at it. There were thirty-three names, and one of them had recommended me to Walt Paddington.

First, I crossed out all the names of people I was pretty sure had no idea I was queer. That left seven names. None of them lived in Carbondale. In fact, all but one lived here in Chicago. Allan Grimley had recently moved to Springfield.

I met Grimley when he ran for the general assembly. He hoped to be the first gay member of the assembly. Instead he got five death threats a day for six weeks. His campaign hired me to consult on security and check out the death threats, since the general consensus was that the police wouldn't bother. It was a nice gig. I got paid a lot of money and managed to keep the guy alive.

When he lost, he got a cushy job lobbying the state for the Chicago Entertainment Association, a group made up largely of bars and restaurants, and ended up moving to Springfield anyway. I put in a call to see if he'd made the recommendation, but ended up talking to his lover, a Cuban boy named Juan who had to be having a rough time in Springfield. He decided to take his anger out on me. I barely got to ask to have Allan call before Juan hung up.

Just for the hell of it, I called the other six names on my list. None of them had recommended me. Two of them pretended not to even remember me.

I headed back up to the north side, picked up the photos, and had coffee and a piece of pie at the Melrose Diner. A cigarette would have been perfect with my coffee, but I had to content myself with watching the other diners smoke. When I was on the job, I could justify the cigarettes with the thought that I risked getting shot every day on the street. I could end up dead anyway, so why worry about cancer? Plus, nicotine helped with the occasional stresses of the street. As a PI, I had fewer justifications.

While I ate my Dutch apple pie à la mode, I re-read Walt's note about Brian and tried to decide if it was any help. The kid liked to drink, so he was probably a regular somewhere. Eugene mentioned The Closet. I put that down as my first stop after I finished my pie. What else? He liked old movies. If I didn't make any progress by Monday I could ask Walt for a list of Brian's favorites, then check them against a Parkway schedule. It was a long shot, but maybe I'd get lucky. Other than that, Walt's note wasn't much use.

The waitress cleared my empty dish, and I asked for a refill on my coffee. I turned Walt's note over and started to make a list of questions I should ask him when he called on Monday. Where did Brian grow up? What's the deal with his parents? Is there a reason he doesn't want Walt to know where he is? How long were they together? How did their relationship start? I began to think there was a whole lot more I didn't know about this kid than I did.

I walked down to The Closet, a tiny bar on Broadway near Buckingham. The dark club held little more than its bar and a space in the back where drinkers milled about. It reminded me of a place from the fifties, when people were serious about their drinking. After showing Brian's picture around to most everyone in the place, I was getting nowhere. I left and decided to hit a few more bars in the area before I headed home to get ready for my shift at Paradise Isle.

The sun set a couple hours before I made it home. I had forty minutes before I needed to get to the club. As I unlocked my door, my mind was working over the whole problem of Brian Peerson. Everything about the case felt wrong. The phone call was funky. The package was weird. Red flags were going up—

When I got to my living room, I saw that the stack of albums that usually sat on the floor next to the stereo was all messed up. As though someone had rifled through them. And, of course, my Thorens turntable and Marantz receiver were gone. The desk where I did my personal bills and worked when I felt like avoiding the office had been rifled, and half my personal files were now on the floor.

I un-holstered my gun, flipped the safety, and went to check out the rest of the apartment. The bedroom was empty, closet door open, clothes thrown about. In the kitchen, the back door stood open. The molding was hanging loose. It opened onto a covered walkway between the sidewalk and the backside of the building. Enjoying their privacy, someone had used a crowbar to pry the door open, and I was going to need both a carpenter and a locksmith to get it working again.

Now that I knew I was alone, I went through the apartment and inventoried what was missing. All my electronics: stereo of course, portable electric typewriter, clock radio, even the freaking toaster. They'd taken some of my clothes. A leather jacket I didn't much like. A couple pairs of pants. Maybe a shirt or two. Nearly fifty bucks I had lying around. The only thing that was going to be a real problem was that they got my spare gun. The Sig is a great gun for walking around. It's small and easy to conceal. But when you know you're going into a bad situation, it's nice to have something a little bigger. Which is why I kept a Smith & Wesson Model 28 with a six-inch barrel in the top drawer of my dresser.

The whole thing stunk of junkies. Professionals don't bother with albums and clothes and small electronics. A professional wouldn't have bothered with me at all. Sure, a garden apartment is easy pickings. But generally there's not much worth picking.

Most people would have called the cops, but there was no way I was doing that. When I did my inventory, I noted that the junkie burglars had missed a half-smoked nickel bag I kept in an old gym shoe and three Quaaludes I had folded in paper and taped up under the bathroom sink. They'd be heartsick if they knew.

And there was no way I was going to let anyone from the CPD wander around my apartment. Sure, I could flush my little stash down the toilet. But that wasn't any guarantee I wouldn't get busted for dope anyway. When it came to Chicago cops, if they knew there was a party they always brought their own.

I'd go by the station on Halsted in a couple days and report the gun stolen. Just to make sure I didn't catch hell if the junkies decided to do something stupid like rob a Walgreen's. I stopped by my upstairs neighbor's. Her name's Sue, and since she's butcher than I am, I figured she'd have a hammer and some nails. She did. I asked her if she'd heard anything during the afternoon, and she scratched her near crew cut and blushed. "I was occupied."

"Well, good for you," I said. I could hardly complain that she was too busy getting laid to hear my break-in. I went ahead and told her what had happened and what had been taken in case I ever needed corroboration.

I found a couple of two by fours in the utility room next to the laundry. It wouldn't do much good, I knew, but I nailed them across my back door anyway. The worst part of it was thinking about the junkie burglars in my place. Looking at my stuff. Making cracks about my taste in music. Giggling over the jack-off magazines on the shelf in my closet. Cracking jokes about why a fag like me had such a cool gun. It felt shitty, and I wanted to punch somebody. Instead, I went to Paradise Isle and watched a couple hundred guys dance the night away.

# # #

I hate Sunday mornings. The fact that I woke up that Sunday at nearly one p.m. didn't change that one iota. Sunday mornings are for couples. Reading the *Sunday Herald.* Making the kind of breakfast your mom made for you when you were a kid. Having lazy sex. I, unfortunately, had to find a carpenter.

Thumping my way out of bed, I put on a pot of coffee and called the company that managed my building. I left word with their service that it was an emergency, and they called me back around the time I was thinking of making a second pot of coffee. The woman, who gave me the impression that my burglary was a bigger problem for her than it was for me, finally gave me the number of a handyman who'd come out on a Sunday and fix my back door.

I was just out of the shower and free-balling it in a pair of gray sweats when the handyman arrived. He said his name was Burt. He stopped in my living room and looked around.

"The door's in the back," I said, not sure why he'd stopped.

"You don't have a TV?"

I shook my head.

"Radio?" he asked.

"It got stolen."

He nodded sympathetically. "Super Bowl today."

Which I would have known, since every male member of the Nowak family lived for the day, except I was living in exile. Sometimes it seemed like a more important holiday than Christmas. I could take football or leave it. I liked the tight uniforms and the quarterback feeling up the center at the start of every play. Other than that it was just a bunch of guys running around being pissed off. I preferred baseball, a game of patience and skill.

Burt headed into the kitchen, where he peeled off his parka and got ready to work. Probably in his early thirties, he wore a white thermal shirt and a pair of blue jean coveralls. He was a faded blond, balding a little, with a killer dimple in the middle of his chin. His body looked to be in great shape: long, ropy muscles covered in fine blond hair. He could probably lift anything in my apartment, including me.

The fact that he was nearly as tall as I was made Ross absolutely wrong about my having a type. Yeah, I liked short, tight little blonds. But once in a while I also liked them tall. Not that I stood a chance with Burt. Even though I kept hanging around the kitchen, bouncing around in my sweats, he didn't notice a thing.

I'm not one of those fags who think every man alive is do-able. This doesn't prevent me from giving a lot of thought to certain unavailable men—like Burt. But it does cut down on the amount of personal rejection I feel, as well as limiting the number of fistfights I end up in. I left Burt to resuscitate my back door and hung around in my living room. I flipped through my albums and made a list of which ones were missing.

Part of me wanted to drop the Peerson thing and figure out who had burgled me. I wasn't exactly sure where junkies hung out in my neighborhood, but I figured if I just walked west four or five blocks I'd probably find some low-life bars. I could go in and spread the word that I was interested in buying my stuff back. It was a long shot, but it might turn something up.

Technically, it was my day off, and I shouldn't feel bad spending it sorting out my B&E. Still, Sunday was the perfect day to spend running around the bars showing Brian Peerson's picture to every queer in the city. I was debating what to do when Burt came into the living room.

"You wanna come look at this?" I wondered if I'd been wrong about him. It was the kind of line that would start a sex scene in a porno. But, when I followed him out to the kitchen, he walked out my back door and led me back to the alley behind the building.

"I was throwing away some wood scraps when I saw that." He pointed halfway down the alley. Next to a garbage can was a smashed turntable that looked suspiciously like mine. I hurried down the alley. Yeah, it was my turntable. And in the trash can next to it I found my clock radio and my toaster. The receiver wasn't there. Either the burglar decided to keep it, or someone else had picked it up during the night.

"That your stuff?"

"Yup." I looked around in a couple more garbage cans and found a shirt and a couple of my albums. The whole thing was beginning to feel more like vandalism than burglary. I had to be honest with myself. In the past couple years I'd run a lot of guys through my bedroom, then asked them to leave without much ceremony. Sometimes the minute we were finished, sometimes the next morning, but they were always asked to leave.

Most didn't mind much, but some were obviously disappointed that I hadn't turned out to be their savior swooping in to rescue them from their shitty childhoods, their mundane jobs in retail, their narrow lives of cigarettes and booze and catty comments. I guess it wasn't too hard to imagine one of them stopping back and taking a stab at making me as unhappy as they were.

Since there never seemed to be a lot of time to get phone numbers between the fucking phase and the please-leave phase, I couldn't exactly call around and find out who I might have pissed off. Which wouldn't be a big deal; I'd just write it off to experience. But this trick with a grudge had stolen my spare gun. That was troubling.

I took my few things and walked back to my apartment. Burt was pretty much finished. A large metal plate now surrounded the deadbolt on my back door. He told me he'd send a bill to the management company and I shouldn't worry about it. When I tried to give him a five, he turned it down. "Keep it. You've had a shitty day."

After Burt left, I had to decide what to do with the rest of my Sunday. I'd reached a dead end on the burglary and didn't expect to come up with any way to nail down whoever did it. At the same time, I was too rattled by it to focus on the Peerson case. I checked the schedule for the

Parkway that sat on top of an unread edition of *The Reader*. They were playing *All About Eve* and *A Shot in the Dark*. It seemed an odd double feature until I remembered that George Sanders was in both of them. I didn't think I had the patience to sit in the dark for four hours, or even two. I could go to the Y, work out some aggression, stop at the bookstore and buy the latest *Blueboy,* then spend the evening jacking off. If I wanted to be productive I could try digging my car out. The '74 Duster had been sitting over on Newport through two snowstorms. If I needed it in a hurry, I'd be in trouble.

In the end, I decided to take a little of Walt Paddington's advance money and go buy a decent boom box. I wandered down Broadway until I found an electronics store whose window was all about Beta-Max VCRs and Video Cameras. Peeking through the soaped-on signage, I saw a small collection of boom boxes. I went in and picked out an off brand player for a hundred and twenty dollars.

Money was tight, and I suppose I shouldn't have bought the boom box, but listening to the tinny sound of my clock radio just wasn't going to cut it. As I walked home in the snow, dragging along the bag with my new boom box, I started thinking about what I had to do the next day. In the morning, I figured I should take some notes about what I'd been doing to find Brian Peerson. Walt Paddington didn't seem the kind who'd want a written report, but I should be clear on what I'd done so far when I spoke to him. Aside from that, I had some background checks to finish up.

When I got back to the apartment, I tuned the boom box to a jazz station and crawled back into bed.

# # #

It was dark when the phone woke me. George Benson was on the radio, and I'd been dreaming about my ex-lover, Daniel. Not my favorite thing. In the dream, I was yelling at him about something. I couldn't remember what. He had a pirate's patch over one eye and didn't bother to yell back. I cursed my subconscious and padded out into the living room, picked up the phone, and grunted into the heavy, black receiver.

"Nick? It's Eugene. You asked me to call if I saw that particular person. Well, he's here at Big Nell's."

Big Nell's is a tiny storefront bar a few blocks from my apartment. They manage to pull in a crowd on Sunday afternoons with a combination of cheap drink specials and Al Parker movies playing on portable TVs dangled from every corner of the bar.

I got there a half hour later, freshly showered and smelling of Polo. Eugene sat at the bar with a couple of very young, very blond men. Twinkies. It took me a minute to be sure, but neither of them was Brian Peerson. I took a stool at the opposite end of the bar and ordered a Miller.

I scanned the bar until I found him. Brian Peerson stood in a huddle with three boys roughly around his age. He wore a dark pair of Calvin Klein jeans, a tight sweater, and a pair of Frey boots with a high enough heel to throw off his posture in a way that flattered his ass. He'd let his hair grow out a little, and the curls were coming back. It was blonder than it had been in his high school photo. He was going for a sun-kissed look, but that didn't happen in Chicago. Not in winter. In winter it looked dyed. He was an attractive kid, but already he was working too hard at it.

His friends seemed to like him, or at least they laughed at his jokes. I wondered a moment what kind of person he was. Then I told myself not to be stupid. All I had to do was wait until he left the bar, follow him home, and get his address. While I waited, I sipped a beer and considered ways to pad my bill so I wouldn't have to send back the part of my retainer I'd just spent on a pumped-up cassette player.

Around eight, Brian grabbed a giant, blue down coat that made him look like the Michelin man when he put it on. I was sure he hadn't noticed me keeping an eye on him. He'd kept his back to me most of the time. Besides, I'd spent the last twenty minutes trying to shake off a drunk guy in his early thirties who was hitting on me pretty hard.

"You sure you don't want to see my place? It's a loft. You know, like they have in New York. It's just fucking great." Brian had just walked out the door. I got off the stool to follow, and the drunk guy grabbed me.

"Listen, listen to me, I'll give you a blow job you'll never forget."

"Yeah," I said. "That's what I'm afraid of."

Before he could think about it, I pulled his hands off me and zipped out the door. Brian was half a block away, heading toward the Addison El stop. Fortunately, the snow had stopped. Everything was covered in a good eight to ten inches, giving the world a muffled quality, like the whole city was suddenly wrapped in gauze. Brian was a good five inches shorter than I am, with shorter legs; I had to be careful not to gain on him.

As we waited on the platform for the train, I hung back out of his line of sight. He smoked a cigarette and cruised a guy on the opposite platform. When the train arrived, I considered getting in the next car in case he recognized me from the bar, but I was afraid I'd lose him. When the doors opened, we both got in; he went one way, I went the other.

We headed north, zipping by Sheridan, Wilson, Lawrence; I began to wonder how far north we'd be going. Finally, he got off at Bryn Mawr. I had to wait until he was well off the train and barely got off without the doors slamming shut on me. Brian wasn't on the platform. Obviously he'd already made it down the stairs.

The area was called Edgewater. It had been nice forty years ago, but now it was seedy and cheap. As evidenced by the train station, which desperately needed renovation. I headed down the stairs. No sign of Brian. He must already be on the street. I picked up my pace to make sure I caught sight of him before he went and turned some corner.

When I spun through the turnstile that put me out onto Bryn Mawr, I was surprised to find Brian standing there, smoking another cigarette. I averted my eyes quickly and turned as though I had a particular destination in mind. My stomach sank when I heard his steps crunching in the snow behind me. He'd figured out I was following him, and now he was returning the favor. I was struggling to figure a way to save the situation when I heard him say, "I know why you've been following me."

I stopped. "Right now you seem to be following me." My mind raced. Had he figured the whole thing out? Did he know Walt was trying to find him? If he knew Walt was looking for him—

"You were at the bar," he said. Then he looked me up and down. It was a look that should have melted the snow around us in a five-foot radius. I smiled. Obviously, he figured I thought he was cute and that's why I was following him home. I decided not to correct him.

He stepped passed me, and I quickly fell into step with him. "Have you lived in this neighborhood long?" I asked.

"Less than a year."

"You like it?"

"Not really. There's a lot of weirdos on the street." He laughed after he said it. Just to let me know he meant me. "Do you have a name?" he asked.

"Nick Nowak."

"I'm Brian Peerson."

I nodded like it was the first time I'd heard the name. We walked a few blocks without saying much, then we turned south on Kenmore. Halfway down the block we stopped in front of a building done up in a Tudor style, like it could have been sitting someplace in Merry Olde England. It was three stories tall, the kind of building that was all studio apartments. I noted the address: 5518.

Brian pushed the security door open. It was broken and no longer required a key. We walked half the length of the building to a small, rickety elevator. After we squeezed in, he pulled the gate shut, and, with a jolt, we began to rise. He seemed nervous. Or maybe I was just projecting. I was nervous, that's for sure. I shouldn't be doing what I was about to do. It violated all sorts of ethical codes, I was sure.

As soon as we got to his apartment door, I'd know his exact address. I should make some excuse and just leave. After all, my client made it seem like he was this kid's boyfriend, and it might even be true. Either way, I knew he wouldn't be too happy about me fucking Brian. Of course, Brian had made it pretty clear he'd be real happy about me fucking him. So it would be hard not to.

When we got into his apartment, number 321, we began to peel off our outer gear. The place was small, about the size of my living room, but cute. Maybe too cute. The walls in the living room were baby blue, and the kitchen was lemon yellow. I couldn't see the bathroom, but I was betting it was pink. There was a mattress and box spring on the floor, a love seat, a desk. One side of the place was all closet doors. Doors that had once flipped open and dropped a Murphy bed.

He had a lot of stuff crammed in there: books, records, prints on the wall. He'd hit the boutiques in New Town pretty hard. All the stuff and the colors he'd picked to paint the place up told me he'd made a home for himself here. Which didn't quite fit with his being on the run from some old boyfriend.

"So, have you got a boyfriend?" I asked. Given the situation, it seemed like a reasonable question.

He looked around the apartment and said, "Where would I put him?" It seemed more evasion than answer, and I wanted to give him a good slap.

Standing on his toes, he kissed me. His lips were still cold from the ride home. He smelled like cigarette smoke and snow and Aramis. He kissed me so deeply I began to wonder how he'd breathe. Then he pulled back and said,

"The minute you walked in the bar, I could tell you were there for me."

So much for my surveillance abilities.

"I love guys like you," he said.

"Really? Why's that?"

He smiled at me and licked his lips. At the same time, he was opening my belt. "Guys like you are easy to figure out."

I don't like being easy to figure out.

Brushing away his hands, I opened up his jeans and yanked them down around his knees. I pulled at his striped bikini briefs until his half-hard cock popped free. It was pink and hooded. Another time I might have enjoyed paying it some attention. Instead, I spun him around and pushed him up against the arch between the living room and the kitchen. I dipped my hand between his ass cheeks and rubbed his hole.

His ass was covered in a light coating of blond hair. I spit on a finger and slipped it into him. Brian wiggled back onto my hand. Deep in his throat he made a rumbling sound, halfway between a whimper and a demand. We were a foot or so away from a little dinette table. A glass dish sat in the middle of the table holding a half stick of butter. I squeezed a chunk and warmed it up in my hands. Quickly, I spread the butter on my dick and all over his ass.

"Ah...Jesus fuck," Brian said as I entered him. I braced myself and began pumping him. I left a buttery handprint on his wall, but I didn't give it a thought. I wasn't thinking about much besides his ass squeezing down on my dick, the shockwaves rippling through his fleshy buttocks, and the panting sighs escaping his lips.

Wrapping both hands around his hips, I pounded into him hard and fast. With each pump I lifted him off the floor so that his cowboy boots tapped against the hardwood floor. I was punishing him, though I couldn't have told you what for.

"Oh my God, oh my God..." Brian groaned.

I picked up speed. A thin layer of sweat broke out over most of my body. With a yelp, I was coming deep inside of him. But still I continued to slam into him until every last drop was squeezed out of me.

Breathing heavily, I stopped and stayed very still for a few moments. I pulled out of him and stepped back. At first, I wasn't sure if he'd come or not. But then, when he stepped away from the wall, I saw that he'd sprayed jizz all over it. When he turned around, there was cum all over the bottom of his sweater, as well.

I noticed he was shaking. A good fuck will do that to you, I thought. But then he turned and looked at the mess we'd made of his wall, cum and buttery handprints everywhere. He took it all in, his neck flushing red with anger.

"I think you'd better leave."

# # #

Before I went down to the Loop the next morning, I bit the bullet and went to report my gun stolen. I walked over a few blocks down to the station at Halsted and Addison. It's a two-story, brick building with over-sized green awnings and a ring of copper embellishing its roofline. It takes up nearly half a block. A white and blue sign hangs off the corner of the building, reading "Chicago Police Department." I tried not to grind my teeth as I climbed the steps into the building.

At the end of the entrance hall, a double door opened onto a squad room. A chest-high front desk blocked entry into the room. Behind the desk, sitting on a stool, was my fat cousin, Jan Duda. He's a good ten years older than I am. Apparently, he finally made sergeant.

I walked up to the desk and said, "I need to file a report."

"You get beat up again?" he asked.

"Burgled."

"Yeah? That's too bad," he said insincerely, as he slid a clipboard my way. There was a pen tied to it with a piece of string and a blank incident report shoved under the clip.

I filled out the report as quickly as I could. I was part way through the inventory of what was taken when Jan asked, "You like sunshine, Nicky?"

"It's got its good points."

"You should move out to San Francisco. They like your kind out there."

"I have roots here."

"Yeah, but your roots don't want you."

I gave him a look that I hoped was cold and withering. He smirked. I went back to working on the report. When I finished, I slid the clipboard back to Jan. He glanced at it, like he wasn't going to bother with it much, but then he stopped.

"You had a gun stolen?" He gave me the cop eye. "Why didn't you call and have someone come over? Give the place the once over."

I gave him a look that said, "You gotta be kidding." He gave it right back to me.

"You're not up to something, are you? Something that would require being disassociated from your own gun."

"I'm a private investigator. Not a criminal."

"Private investigator. A noble profession," he said in a way that meant the opposite.

I walked out of the station and broke my New Year's resolution by picking up a pack of cigarettes at a little shop next to the El. Marlboro Reds in a box. Then I stood on the Addison platform and smoked half a dozen cigarettes while I watched the trains go by. Each time I inhaled it felt like a toddler kicking me in the chest. God, I'd missed smoking.

The unreasonable part of me wanted to get a semi-automatic weapon and blow away every cop in the city. The reasonable part just wanted to limit the destruction to my family members. San Francisco. No, that wasn't for me. I'd miss the suspense of wondering which of my toes had frostbite.

I finally hopped a train and made my way to my office. Nearby, I picked up a grilled ham and cheese, an extra greasy order of fries, and a Pepsi. When I unwrapped the sandwich, the cheese stuck to the paper. Meticulously, I scraped it off and put it back onto the sandwich. It was delicious and gone in four minutes flat.

I lit a cigarette and thought, "If there is a God, he's a son of a bitch. If he wanted to do us a favor he would have made raw carrots and bean sprouts as appealing as a fatty, fried sandwich and a Marlboro."

At 2:11, Walt Paddington hadn't called. Something was off about him. I'd felt that from the start. I just didn't know what. Of course, when he did finally call, I'd let him know I found Brian and give him the kid's address. That was my job. That's what I'd been paid to do. That's the deal I'd struck. But I was starting to feel bad about it.

The phone rang at 2:27. Even though I was expecting it to ring, I jumped. "Mr. Nowak?"

"Mr. Paddington."

"Yes. Yes, it's me." He had the same nervous quality I'd noticed the first time I talked to him. Except now it seemed fake, although I didn't know exactly why. "Please tell me you have good news for me."

"How's Carbondale? Snowing down there?"

"I...I don't know, haven't been outside."

"You don't have windows?"

"I have curtains. Which are closed. Mr. Nowak, I didn't call to talk about the weather—"

"Radio said you guys got hit pretty hard." They didn't say that on the radio. In fact, they said the opposite. The state was snow-free for the first time in a week.

"Okay, yeah, I just took a peek and it's coming down pretty bad. There's a good four inches on the ground. Did you find Brian?"

"Yes. I did."

"Excellent work. Let me get a pen, then you can give me his address." The phone went silent. I wanted to find a way out of giving him the address. It was really just a hunch, but it was a strong one. Paddington came back on the line, "Okay, I'm ready."

"Why don't you give me your address first?" I suggested.

"What for?"

"Well, I didn't use the entire retainer," I cursed myself for saying it. It meant I'd have to return my boom box. "I should send a final invoice and a check for the difference."

"You did this pretty fast. I appreciate that. Why don't you keep the rest as a bonus?"

"You don't want to give me your address. Why not?"

The line went silent. "If I don't give you my address, you're not giving Brian's. Is that the deal?"

"Maybe." And maybe it was. I hadn't thought this out.

"I paid for that address. If you don't give it to me, it's a kind of theft." He paused, and then hit me with, "Maybe I'll call the cops. Tell them you stole from me. You don't like it when people call the cops, do you?"

The cops wouldn't bother with something like this. But they would bother with me, and he seemed to know that. He seemed to know a lot.

"What do you know?" I whispered.

"I know that you're going to give me Brian's address like a good boy."

I was quiet for a long time. Then I gave him Brian's address. Not because he knew stuff about me, not because he was messing with me, but because he was right. He'd paid for the information. It was his. If I wasn't willing to give clients the information they'd paid for, well, then I'd have to find a different way to make a living.

He repeated the address back to me and then, without saying goodbye, hung up.

I sat there holding the receiver numbly in my hand and slipped into my past. I didn't want to think about it, I come from people who say 'what's done is done' and move on. But when some asshole who shouldn't know a thing about you starts hinting that he knows all your secrets... Well, what else are you going to think about?

We'd been together almost three years, Daniel Laverty and I. He was small, blond, and tightly muscled. I guess if I have a type, it's because of Daniel. His eyes were the blue of a summer sky that clouded over whenever I made him unhappy. He had a way of laughing at me when I was mad that made everything I did or said seem silly. And he had a hundred ways of saying my name; ways that meant he loved me, that he expected more from me, that I was perfect, or awful, or just too ridiculous to take seriously. It was the best almost-three years of my life.

Daniel had a friend who did a drag show at a bar on Sheffield. The bar closed a year or so ago. People called it Mary's, but I'm pretty sure that wasn't the actual name of the place. It might have been the name two or three owners ago, but it definitely wasn't the night we went.

I don't remember the friend's real name, but his drag name was Candy Caine. I also remember I didn't want to go. Not only is drag not exactly my thing, but as a police officer the last place I wanted to be seen was in a gay bar. I was afraid someone might spot me going in, or catch me going out. I was afraid I might even see someone I knew from the job in the bar. Sure, if I ran into another cop in a gay bar we were in the same boat. But paranoia is paranoia. It's not exactly rational.

Daniel wanted to go, though, and was willing to fight with me most of the day to make it happen. It was summer. Hot. Muggy. And he finally wore me down. When I got to the bar, I hit the booze pretty hard to keep my discomfort in check. Did a bunch of shots. Drank lots of beers. By the time the show was over, I was drunk. I used to be one of those people who get overly affectionate when they drink too much. It always embarrassed Daniel, since I'd do insincere shit like telling Candy Caine she actually looked like a woman, so he steered me out of Mary's before I could get too sloppy.

We were cutting over on Cornelia to get to Halsted. The street was dark. One two-story courtyard apartment building followed the next. I slipped my hand around Daniel's waist. I pulled him close to me. He chuckled a little, happy to get the rare bit of PDA out of me.

"You're gonna feel like crap in the morning," he said.

I don't know where they came from. Four of them. They looked like kids from one of the better suburbs. Other than that, I couldn't tell you much about them. They got between us. Calling names. Talking shit. I went into cop mode and tried to defuse the situation. Warning them off, which only caused two of them to start poking their fingers into my chest.

Out of the corner of my eye, I saw another of the guys bouncing an aluminum bat in his hand. Twitching almost. Getting ready to swing. Daniel was yelling. I sensed the situation slipping into chaos. I reached for a gun I wasn't wearing. Bat Boy reared back to swing. Frustrated, I grunted as I jumped for him. But the two who'd been poking at me grabbed me, while the fourth swung a punch into my stomach. The bat arced and caught Daniel square in the left cheek.

Down on the ground, screaming, Daniel holding his face.

Rage ripped through me like a wildfire. I kicked at the guys holding me, which made it hard for the one throwing punches. I wiggled and twisted trying to get away from them. Individually, I could have pounded the crap out of them. But working together, they had the upper hand.

The one with the bat stood over Daniel. He looked like he was going to take another swing. "No!" I yelled.

Suddenly, Bat Boy got hit in the face with what turned out to be a potato. He stepped away from Daniel and looked around. A voice from above yelled, "Leave them alone you sons of bitches." A couple more potatoes flew by. This gave me an in, and I was able to pull away from the two guys holding onto me. I spun around, wind-milling my arms, and caught one of them in the chin. He went down.

Between my lucky punch and the potatoes that continued to connect every so often, the guys started looking at each other. One of them said, "Fuck it. Let's get out of here."

The whole thing took two, three minutes tops. But it felt like it went on forever. They were gone, running down the street. Daniel was still screaming. Had screamed the whole time. I bent down over him.

"It's okay. They're gone."

He took a couple of deep breaths and said, "Hurts like fuck." He started moaning after that. Loud. But at least it wasn't a scream.

"Sweetie," came the voice from above. "You want me to call the cops or get an ambulance?"

I turned around and for the first time looked at the guy who'd help us out of this mess. He was a queen in his sixties. His fire-engine red kimono hung open as he leaned out the window, revealing chalk-white skin and an emaciated frame.

"No, don't do that," I told him, flushed with embarrassment. I should have been able to handle this, I told myself—as I would tell myself again and again.

"You sure? Your friend doesn't seem okay."

"We're fine," I snapped. "Mind your own business."

The queen swore at me and slammed his window shut.

I pulled Daniel off the ground. He held his hand tightly over his left cheek and eye. I started walking him down the street. I didn't feel drunk anymore. In fact, I felt completely clear-headed.

"We'll get a cab and go to the hospital," I told Daniel. "Just tell them you fell down and hit your head on the curb. We've been drinking. They'll believe it."

We reached Halsted, and I stepped out into the street to hail a cab. Luckily, there was one a block away. After we climbed in and I told the driver to take us to Illinois Masonic, Daniel got very quiet. I was glad the moaning had stopped. But I wasn't prepared when he said, "I'm going to tell the truth."

"What?"

"I'm not going to tell people I fell down. That's not what happened."

"You can't do that. They'll call the police."

"So, we just let them get away with it?" he asked.

"What do you think the police are going to do? Some kids beat up a couple of fags. You think that's a high priority?"

"If we don't report it, nothing will ever change."

"You know what will happen to my job."

"They can't fire you. Can they?"

"They don't have to fire me. Once people know, I'm not going to want to be there."

"You're overreacting."

Daniel didn't understand. The guys I worked with, a lot of them had been on the job going back to the sixties. They talked about raiding fag bars like it was the good old days. Like they were pissed they didn't get to push a bar full of fruits into a paddy wagon anymore. Hell, the way my family was, my Christmas presents when I was a kid were probably bought with payoff money from the fag bars they didn't raid.

How was I going to work with these people if they knew I'd been bashed with my boyfriend? And they would know. There was no way we could report this with them not knowing. Everything would be over. I wouldn't be able to be a cop anymore.

"We're going to tell everyone you fell," I repeated.

Daniel didn't respond.

The cabbie pulled up in front of the emergency room entrance at Illinois Masonic. Daniel got out of the cab under his own steam, and I paid the driver. I walked into the waiting room, looked around, and found Daniel standing in a short line waiting to check in. I walked over and stood next to him.

He looked at me and dropped his hand from his left eye. His cheek was enormous, his eye swollen shut, oozing in a way that looked bad.

"Coward," he whispered.

"Daniel, I did everything I could. There were four of them. If I'd had my gun—"

"I'm not talking about that."

The woman at the desk called him over, took one look at his eye, and pointed at the double doors he needed to go through.

"You want me to go with you?" I asked.

But he never answered. Instead he just walked through the double doors. Fifteen minutes later an officer walked in, talked to the woman at the desk, and then followed the same path Daniel had taken. I waited a moment, then left.

I never saw Daniel again. He reported what had happened. An Officer Reilly caught me one morning before my shift, and even though I refused to talk about it, the story got around. Things got bad. I resigned two weeks later. During my last shift, Daniel let himself into our apartment and took his stuff. Leaving holes I never bothered to fill.

I thought the harassment would stop when I quit the department. It didn't. I get stopped two or three times a month. Driving too fast. Driving too slow. Failing to signal. I've gotten tickets for busted taillights that weren't busted when I was stopped. I even got a ticket for driving with an open container, said container was thoughtfully provided by one Officer Jankowitz. If I go down to the courthouse to fight the tickets, the cops never show up, so I get off and I don't have to pay. But it's a pain in my ass, and that's the point.

Walt Paddington had shaken me up, and I wasn't going to sit still for it. I had to do something, but I wasn't sure what. I needed more information. I pulled out a file and looked up a phone number. Dialed.

"Hello, Juan, this is Nick Nowak. Is Allan there?"

An angry silence told me he was.

"Can I talk to him?"

The phone was dropped on some kind of table, and there were some snappish voices in the background. Then Allan came onto the phone, "Nick! It's *so* good to hear from you." Allan was one of those politicians who couldn't turn it off. The kind who, if he gave you a blow job, would ask for your vote afterward. "What can I do for you?"

"Did you recommend me to a guy named Walt Paddington?" I asked.

"No, I don't think so."

"You don't think so? You either did or you didn't?"

"Hold on a second. I need to take this in the other room."

The receiver went crash on the table again. A moment or two later, another line was picked up. Then Allan and Juan yelled at each other until Juan reluctantly hung up the extension.

"I don't know why he's like this. I go to a bar and he freaks out. But it *is* really part of my job. I have to know who's who and what the latest trends—"

"So, you recommended me to someone in a bar?"

He sighed heavily, already realizing he'd screwed up. "Yeah, this guy was asking if anyone knew a gay private eye in Chicago. I was doing you a *favor*."

"By telling him my life story?"

He paused. "I'd had a few drinks. I'm sorry."

"What did he look like?"

"Older. Balding. Little heavy around the middle, I guess. Really, he seemed like the most harmless guy." He waited for me to agree. "Nick, what's going on? Did I mess up?"

"Anything weird about him? Anything you remember."

Allan thought for a moment. "He seemed out of place. Like he'd never been in a gay bar before and expected everyone to jump him."

"Closet case?"

"That's what I thought at first. But... I mean, now that you're calling me, I don't know. He left right after I gave him your info. Maybe he wasn't gay."

I thanked him and hung up. I took out a scratch pad and wrote down what I'd just learned. The guy who hired me lived in Springfield, or somewhere in that area. He probably wasn't gay, so the story he'd implied about Brian was crap. I figured there was a ninety-nine point nine percent chance his name wasn't really Walt Paddington. I made a note on my to-do list to check that out—though it wasn't a high priority. If he didn't want to give me his address, it seemed unlikely he'd given me his real name. The only two things I knew for sure were that he wanted Brian's address and he didn't want me to know who or where he was. I didn't like that. I didn't like it all.

Technically, I was finished with the job. I was supposed to respect my client's privacy and stop investigating. I was supposed to move on and forget whatever I'd learned. After my call with Allan Grimley, there was no way I was doing that.

# # #

I took the El back up to my neighborhood and walked over to Newport. The Plymouth was buried so deep under the snow that you could barely tell it was blue. Using my hands, I pushed enough snow off the trunk so I could open it. I got out the brushes and the snow shovel I kept there. It wasn't just the snow that had fallen on the car that was the problem. The plow had been by a few times and had packed a thick layer of snow along the driver's side.

The call from Paddington, or whatever his name was, had the faint, crackling sound long distance calls sometimes have. Chicago is a couple hundred miles from Springfield. In the summer it would take three, three and a half hours to drive it. The roads were clear, but leftover snow and a patch or two of ice along the way would slow the drive down a bit. Whatever Paddington was planning would take preparation. Yeah, I knew he might not be at home in Springfield, but my gut said he wasn't in Chicago. He'd be here soon, though. I had to move and move quickly

Thirty minutes later, I'd managed to get my car dug out of its spot. Thankfully, it started on the third try. I had to rock it back and forth a few times and finally resort to slipping an old piece of cardboard under the back tires. It tore up the cardboard, and I reminded myself to grab another old box sometime. In Chicago, you had to be prepared. I weaved through a couple of blocks until I worked my way to Broadway, then took Broadway north to Bryn Mawr.

When I got close to Kenmore, I prayed that there was a parking spot within sight of Brian's building. I'd forgotten that Kenmore was one way, so I spun around the block and came at Brian's place from the south. I found a parking place toward the end of the block. I couldn't really see his building from there, so I'd have to keep my eyes open for a better spot. It was a little after five, and the sky was turning gray.

Surveillance in the winter is a bitch. My gas tank was three quarters full, so I'd be able to run the engine every so often to get a little heat. I got a blanket and pillow out of the trunk, kept for occasions just like this. Not that I did this kind of thing often. Whenever possible, I avoided it.

At six, I walked down to Bryn Mawr and looked around until I found Helios' Gyros, a small, storefront Greek place that specialized in take out. It looked to be Helios himself working the grill and cutting lamb strips off a big hunk of compressed meat on a metal spit. Helios had curly black hair trying to escape his undershirt and looked to be covered with sweat. You sort of hoped he didn't get too close to your food. I bought a gyros and a big Styrofoam cup of coffee to go.

Huddled in my car, I kept my eyes glued to the side mirror, which was really the only way I could see any of Brian's building. The car stunk of lamb, even though I swallowed my dinner in six bites. About a half hour later I a panel van left a parking spot closer to Brian's place and I managed to get around the block in time to snag the spot. That put me about three buildings south, on the east side of the street. I could easily see Brian's front door without having to twist around or use any mirrors. It was exactly where I wanted to be.

For the next couple hours, I kept my eyes peeled for balding, middle-aged guys with spare tires. Of course, the description didn't make him sound exactly dangerous. But that's one thing I learned back when I was on the job; dangerous people don't always look that way. Hell, sometimes the scariest person on your block is the gray-haired granny who can't quite stand up straight.

Around nine o'clock, Brian came home. He was bundled up tight in his blue down jacket, but his pants were black and his shoes looked sensible. I figured he was wearing a white shirt underneath. Coming home from work. I figured he was in for the night. Monday wasn't a big night for going out. It was the night you recovered from everything you did over the weekend and began storing up your energy for Thursday when the weekend began. If you lived in the city, you hit the popular places on Thursday night to avoid the suburbanites who came in on Friday and Saturday. Then on Friday and Saturday, you went to the places they hadn't discovered yet.

The night was long and cold. Every once in a while I got out of the car and walked around. Whenever I was sitting in the Plymouth, I tried to look like some guy down on his luck or at least someone not too threatening. Made me wish I did harmless a whole lot better. The last thing I needed was for one of the neighbors to call the cops. Given half a chance, they'd arrest me for loitering. Hell, they'd probably book me for solicitation just to get a good laugh.

On my walks, I picked up another couple cups of coffee at Helios' and sucked them down. Still, I fell asleep around four and didn't wake up until just before eight. I was glad no one was paying me for this; I'd have felt guilty. Of course, if Paddington had slipped into Brian's building and done whatever it was he was planning, I might end up feeling guilty anyway.

Or maybe I was I just overreacting. Maybe there was a perfectly normal explanation and I wasn't seeing it. And if there was, I was going to end up feeling damn stupid. Still, I'd rather be humiliated than know someone got hurt while I did nothing. I did know one thing; I couldn't spend another night on the street. I had to come up with a better plan.

After an hour of debating, I went down to my new favorite restaurant and bought a couple cups of coffee and some baklava. I headed back to Brian's building and let myself in through the busted security door. A couple minutes later, I was knocking on Brian's door. The reception I got when he answered was about what I was expecting: "What do you want?"

He was wearing a towel, obviously fresh from the shower. I hadn't seen much of his body before, and I have to be honest, I liked what I was seeing. His pectorals were like smooth slabs on his chest, and he tapered nicely into a tight little waist. A little tuft of hair began above his navel and ran into the towel. All in all, it was nice to see him again. I didn't even mind the nasty look he was giving me. It was the look you give a trick when he shows up uninvited. I'd given that look a few times myself.

"I brought you coffee and some baklava," I said.

"I'm not hungry."

"I've got something important to tell you."

Curiosity wrinkled his forehead. He didn't like the seriousness in my voice. I could almost read his thoughts. We'd only had sex two days ago. There hadn't been enough time for me to discover I'd given him some annoying venereal disease I'd come to apologize for.

"I'm a private investigator. I was hired to find you."

He looked at me for a moment. "What exactly is baklava?"

"Pastry. Soaked in honey and sprinkled with nuts."

He stepped to one side and let me into the apartment. It was warm, stuffy even. After my night in the car, it was a relief, though at that point I would have enjoyed the Sahara at high noon. The apartment looked freshly cleaned—now I knew what Brian did on his Monday nights. I glanced at the spot we'd christened on the wall. A lot of scrubbing had gone on, but hadn't helped much.

I handed Brian a sticky piece of baklava and a coffee. The tiny dinette table in front of his kitchen window was from the fifties, all chrome and bright yellow vinyl. He sat in one chair, I took the other.

"I was hired to find you. The guy called me on the phone, said he was from a particular city downstate, but he's not." I wasn't supposed to divulge client information, and technically I hadn't. My client hadn't given me this information. "A guy I know in Springfield recommended me to a middle-aged, balding gentleman, thick around the waist."

Brian picked at his baklava, but didn't eat it.

"This sound like anyone you know?"

"I appreciate your coming by, but I've got to get ready for work..."

"In other words, you do know him."

"Not that it's any of your business, but I grew up in Springfield. My mother still lives there. With her husband." He got up and walked into the main room. He dropped the towel onto the bed and walked naked into the large closet.

I noted that he'd said 'her husband,' meaning his mother was not married to his father. He came out of the closet still naked but carrying his waiter's uniform. "Where's your father live?" I asked.

"He doesn't. He died when I was five." He slipped on the black slacks.

"So, you think it's your stepfather who's looking for you?"

"Look, this is a family thing. He probably wanted my address so my mom could write me a letter. It's not a big deal. You didn't have to come by."

"What's your stepfather's name?"

"I think you know that."

"Actually, I think I don't."

"Donnie Carr."

"That's not the name he gave me."

Brian shrugged his way into the white shirt. "I told you. This isn't a big deal."

"If it's not a big deal, why use a fake name?"

"That's just the way he is. He's the sort of person who tells a lie even when there's nothing wrong with the truth. It's his thing."

I waited. He wanted to get rid of me; that was easy to figure. But I wasn't going anywhere until I knew what was what. It took a minute for him to figure that out.

"My mother had breast cancer a few years ago. I was a junior in high school. She had surgery. Radiation. Some chemo that made her pretty sick. She started going to this church. I went a couple of times. It was...intense. Real bible-thumpers. She met Donnie there. She thought he was a wonderful guy because he didn't care about her not having breasts anymore. When they told her she was okay again, she married him."

He attached a black cummerbund around his waist, then slipped a matching clip-on bow tie in his shirt pocket.

"I went away to college. Everything was okay until I got my first boyfriend. I thought I was in love, thought it was going to last forever, so I wrote my mother a letter telling her all about my boyfriend. I didn't think...I'm an only child. It had been just my mom and me for a really long time. I never thought she wouldn't want to see me anymore. But that's Donnie. And the church they go to."

"You said he's a liar."

"He's a sales rep. Liquor, I think. He told my mother he made a lot more money than he actually did. He played it like he had money to spare, but after they got married she found out he didn't have much. She also found out he had an ex-wife and a kid he was paying child support on." He grabbed the big, blue coat. "I'm going to be late for work if I don't leave now."

"Let's go then." He frowned at me, then led me out of the apartment. When we got to the street, I asked, "Where do you work?"

"Down in the Loop. You're not going to follow me to work, are you?"

"It's a free country." I didn't know what I was going to do, but I'd feel better if I knew Brian was okay. "You think your stepfather would hurt anyone?"

"Only my mother."

"He beats her?"

"No, emotionally. He hurts her emotionally." We'd gotten to the El station. Brian stopped in front of the turnstile. "Look I appreciate your trying to warn me, or whatever, but you can't follow me around all day. Okay?"

We rode the El down to the Loop and got off at Madison. Brian worked at a restaurant near there called the French Bakery. It was a two-story storefront at the bottom of a fifteen-story granite building from the thirties. There was a Florsheim on one side and a brand-new copy shop on the other. Before we went in, he threatened to call the police if I set foot in the restaurant, so I let him go in alone. I looked at the shoes in the Florsheim window for five minutes. Then I went in.

On the first floor there was a bakery selling all the traditional French goodies: elephant ears, napoleons, éclairs. Upstairs at the front there was a bar on a kind of mezzanine that looked out onto Madison and down on the bakery. In the back was a restaurant and kitchen. To one side, as you came up the stairs, was a picture window where you could watch actual French bakers making croissants by buttering dough and pushing it through a roller over and over again.

I went into the bar and ordered a coffee. The barmaid looked at me suspiciously for a moment, so I asked her to throw in a shot of Kahlua. At eleven-thirty I asked for a menu and ordered some lunch. The bar was beginning to fill up, and I thought I'd get my order in before it got too crowded. The barmaid took my order. Her name was Sheila, and she seemed unnecessarily friendly. I wanted a grilled ham and cheese on rye, but the only thing close was a brie omelet with a baguette.

After all the coffee I'd had in the last twenty-four hours, my bladder was sending some painful signals. I wandered around until I found the men's room. Next to it was a payphone, and it got me thinking. When I was done, I came out and dug around in my pocket for some change. I called information in Springfield and got the number for Donnie Carr. I dialed, then dumped in the eight-five cents the operator wanted for three minutes.

A woman answered. I didn't really know what I was going to say, so I just jumped in. "Mrs. Carr?"

She left a pause. "No, this isn't Mrs. Carr. Who's this?"

"Can I speak to Mrs. Carr?"

"Who's calling please?"

"I'm a friend of her son Brian."

There was a gasp at the other end of the line. "Do you know where he is?"

"Yes, yes, I do."

"She wants to see him again. She wants to see him so much."

"I'll let him know." And I would, too.

"No. He needs to come right away. If you could give—"

"Has something happened?"

"Please, could you give me Brian's phone number? Mr. Carr said he's done everything to find him. I don't think that's true."

"Where is Mr. Carr?"

"He's not here. Please, the number. The news should come from me. I've been cleaning for them for almost twenty years. I used to babysit Brian. He was such a sweet—"

"What's happened to Mrs. Carr?"

She hesitated a moment, then, "The cancer came back. So fast. Her lungs. Her liver. There isn't much time—" The woman's voice broke. It took her a moment to get hold of herself. "I'm only here because Mr. Carr asked me to pack up her things. He wants to give her things to charity. She isn't even dead yet."

"Where did you say Mr. Carr was?"

"I didn't." I'd pushed too hard, and she'd become cautious.

She needed a nudge, so I gave it to her. "Seems awful cold, him rushing things like that. Disrespectful."

"He's in Indianapolis. On a sales trip." The way she spat the words out gave a good indication what she thought of him. "She's been in the hospital for weeks. He's barely taken a day off. Please, please give me Brian's phone number."

I made up a number and gave it to her. Partly because I didn't know Brian's phone number, and partly because I wanted to be the one to decide when he found out his mother was dying.

Back in the bar, my omelet was waiting for me. It was cold. As I began eating, Brian came into the bar and put in an order at the service bar. When he saw me, he gave me a look that was colder than my omelet. If he didn't like me now, how much was he going to hate me when I told him his mother was dying?

The place did a good business. By one o'clock it was full, and people were starting to line up, waiting to get in. A blackboard over the host's station told you why. They had a soup and salad special for under three bucks. The place was a secretary's delight.

The omelet had made me a little sick to my stomach, which was a good enough reason to order another Kahlua and coffee. I looked out the window and saw that it had started to snow again, pretty heavily. I thought about Donnie Carr. I took all the pieces of the puzzle apart again and put them back together. They came out the same. He wasn't in Indianapolis. Sure, he might have gone over this morning, checked into a hotel, made a few sales calls, called around and made some appointments for tomorrow. Sometime this evening he'd be in Chicago.

I could see what he was doing. Constructing an alibi. If something happened to Brian, no one could prove Donnie knew where he was. And no one could prove he wasn't in Indianapolis. He was coming to kill his stepson. That was the only thing that made sense. I tried to see it another way. He just wanted to talk? He wanted Brian to come home to see his mother? But none of that made sense with all the deception. Only murder made sense.

The thing I didn't know was why Donnie wanted to kill Brian. Typically, these things were about sex or money. Even though I'd never met Donnie Carr, everything I'd heard about him made me think he was the kind of guy who liked money more than sex.

Brian's shift ended at three. I'd had four Kahlua and coffees, and I was a little loose on my feet following him down the stairs and out of the restaurant. When we got out to Madison, he turned on me. "How do I get rid of you?"

"Let's take a cab home. I don't think I can deal with the train."

"I want you to go away. Why are you not getting that?"

"I think you're in danger."

"Yeah, I know. My stepfather has my address. I'm shaking in my boots." He looked at the snow falling. I could see in his face he wasn't much interested in waiting on a cold and snowy platform for a train that might not even have heat. I saw a Checker cab coming and raised my hand to flag it.

After I gave the cabbie Brian's address, I asked Brian, "What's the deal with your real father?"

"I told you, he's dead."

"Did he leave a lot of money?"

"I suppose. My mom never had to work, and then she paid for my college. Until I told her I was gay."

"She cut you off?"

"Not exactly." He looked out the window and watched the traffic crawl by, but he kept talking. "She wanted me to go to this psychiatrist who promised to fix me. She'd only pay my tuition if I went. I think it was Donnie's idea, or maybe the shrink's, I don't know. She'd never been like that about anything."

"Do you know what happens to the money?"

"What do you mean what happens to it?"

"If something happens to your mother. Who gets the money?"

"Why is that your business?"

"I didn't say it was my business. I'm trying to figure something out."

"There's nothing to figure out. My stepfather wanted my address so he and my mother can send me religious pamphlets telling me I'm going to hell. Big fucking deal."

"Brian, your mother is dying."

He snapped his head to look at me and then narrowed his eyes. "How would you know that?"

"I called your house. I spoke to the maid. The cancer returned. It's in your mother's liver, her lungs."

"You're lying."

"We can call. I don't know if the maid will still be there. She said she was just packing up your mother's things."

"What's the maid's name?"

"I don't know. She didn't say."

"You're lying," he said again. But the tears forming in his eyes suggested that he believed me. "So that's why Donnie's looking for me. He wants to tell me she's sick."

"What happens to the money, Brian?"

He shrugged and then rubbed his hands across his eyes. "It's mine, I guess."

"And if something happens to you? Before your mother passes?"

"I don't know. It's not like we sat around the house reading wills all the time." His chin was wobbling, and he'd start sobbing soon. I could tell he didn't want to do it in front of me.

"If something happens to you, Donnie gets the money. Isn't that right?" It was the final piece of the puzzle. It had to be the reason.

"Probably. I don't know."

"Donnie knows. He's going to try and kill you. Tonight."

# # #

Brian didn't believe me. That happens sometimes. Some things are too big to take in and a person decides it can't be true, no matter how obvious it is. Denial, they call it. And to be fair, I didn't have a lot of proof. I had a lot of conjecture, logical, sound conjecture—but easy enough to ignore.

The cab pulled up in front of his apartment building, and Brian turned to me. "If you get out of the cab, I'm gonna call the police." He glared at me a second, then added, "I mean it."

I figured this time he did. I would have preferred to stick close, but I'd said what I needed to say, and if he didn't want me around, then he didn't want me around. He got out, and I told the cabbie to drive around the block. When we came around again, Brian had gone into his building. I had the driver let me out in front of my Plymouth. I tried to calculate when Donnie might arrive. He'd want to be seen around Indianapolis as late as possible. It was getting close to four o'clock. Donnie was already on his way, I bet. Given traffic and the snow that was continuing to fall. I guessed he'd be at Brian's door sometime between eight and nine o'clock. I had a nice long wait in front of me.

I ran the engine for a while to get the heat going. It steamed up the windows, but I didn't care. Brian wouldn't be coming out of his apartment anytime soon. The poor kid was probably crying his eyes out over his dying mother. He might even be calling around Springfield trying to find out what hospital she was in, hoping all the while I'd been telling him an elaborate lie. I turned on the radio and checked the weather.

The storm was going to be big. The lake effect was kicking in. It was going to be bad. What I really needed was some sleep. I wrapped the blanket around me and turned off the engine. I told myself it was safe to take a nap for an hour or so. But whenever I closed my eyes, they'd pop back open and I'd find myself staring at Brian's front door. I second-guessed myself for the next couple hours. There was something bothering me, and it took me awhile to put my finger on it. Donnie had gone to a lot of trouble to find me, to find a gay PI. But had he needed to? Really? Couldn't anyone have gotten him the address? Suddenly, I was back at the beginning; back to my very first question—why me?

Around seven, I walked down to Helios' Gyros and got a large coffee and a gyros. Helios wasn't there. Someone else was cooking, but he was just as hairy and greasy as Helios, so I figured the gyros would be pretty good. I paid for my order and took the Styrofoam cup of coffee in one hand and the foil-wrapped gyros in the other. I slipped a couple napkins into my pockets and was back on the street.

I was part way down Kenmore and thinking I really needed to get some variety in my diet, when I saw them come out of Brian's building: Brian and a man who fit the description I had of Donnie. They turned and headed south. I kicked myself, and had a couple of good reasons to do it. One, Donnie had been there waiting for Brian to come home from work. I'd completely blown it on the ETA front. Two, I'd been off getting a sandwich. If they'd come out a couple minutes earlier, I would have missed them completely. It was just dumb luck I hadn't.

I couldn't tell if Donnie looked like his description or not. He was wearing a knit hat, a leather jacket that was far too large for him, and a pair of pants that was bunched up around his ankles. There was something wrong about that, but I couldn't think what. Donnie was walking real close behind Brian. Close enough that he probably had a gun. I flashed back to my police training and ran through protocol. Protocol said call for backup.

Unfortunately, I didn't have a CB radio in my car. Not that the police would come if they knew it was me. I suppose I could have run for a payphone and called the cops from there, but in the time it took me to do that, Donnie and Brian could be anywhere in a three-block radius. I could have stopped a passerby and asked them to call the cops, but again, who knew where we'd be by the time they arrived. No, it was up to me to deal with the situation.

Donnie's clothes continued to bug me. There was something familiar about them. And they were clearly the wrong size. I nearly slapped myself in the head when I realized the clothes were mine. It was Donnie who'd broken into my apartment a few days back. Not some junkie. Not some psycho-trick. Donnie. And that meant he had my Smith & Wesson tucked into the small of Brian's back.

Reaching into my coat, I flipped the safety on my Sig.

When they got to Foster, Donnie and Brian turned east toward the lake. The snow fell heavy and fast, fast enough that there was a good four to five inches coating the streets. The world seemed muffled, as though we'd all gone a little deaf.

Lincoln Park runs up and down the lakeshore on the north side. Certain parts, like the parking lot at Foster Beach, a thicket of bushes further to the south, and the Belmont rocks, were known to be cruisy. Donnie was taking Brian over to the parking lot for Foster Beach, which was just beyond the underpass he and Brian were now walking through.

Somewhere in the parking lot or the trees nearby he was going to shoot Brian. With my gun. In my clothes—clothes he'd make sure to get Brian's blood on. Then he'd walk away. He'd change the clothes somewhere. His car maybe. Then stash the clothes and the gun somewhere they were sure to be found. Like in a garbage can behind my apartment building.

Well, that answered the 'why me' question. Donnie's plan came into focus. Find a gay PI to dig up Brian's address, then frame him for Brian's murder. Economical. Elegant even. Killing Brian in a known cruising spot would make the police think it was some sick, psychosexual thing. They'd find me pretty quick. Possibly through an anonymous tip. I'd tell them I'd been hired to find Brian. By a client I couldn't produce.

As we approached the parking lot, I noticed there were half a dozen cars. That was a surprise. The wind had picked up, and it continued to snow heavily. These were not guys out for an evening stroll. These were guys sitting in their cars trying to meet other guys sitting in their cars, or better— walking by. I couldn't believe it. I've done a lot of stupid things trying to get laid, but this seemed extreme.

I think the cars were a surprise to Donnie as well, because he turned Brian toward the beach. Roughly forty feet separated us. He hadn't noticed me, yet. He would eventually. Of course, he'd have no idea who I was. Even when I got close.

The beach was covered in a foot of snow. I wouldn't even have known I was on the sand if the ground beneath my feet hadn't suddenly seemed to soften and shift. Donnie was looking from side to side. He didn't want to shoot Brian on the beach. Too open, too visible to the cars in the parking lot. Several of which had their lights on. He seemed to make a decision and turned Brian suddenly to the right.

In that direction, there was a small pier with a thirty-foot-tall beacon at the end. The beacon was made of sheets of steel for the first fifteen feet and then crisscrossing girders after that. A light at the top spun slowly around. Ice had formed at the edge of the beach and all around the pier.

Seeming all too aware of what was about to happen, Brian abruptly tried to pull away from Donnie. But Donnie kept hold of him, and I caught a glimpse of my Smith & Wesson as Donnie brought it up to Brian's face and held it there. Brian stopped struggling, and Donnie pushed him forward.

I picked up my pace, trying to close the distance between us. The wind was driving waves of water over the pier, and I wanted to get to them before they reached it. I started to run, but lost my footing in snow-covered sand. I got up as quickly as possible and trudged on. Moments later, they were at the pier. Brian was resisting again.

"Good boy," I muttered to myself. "Slow him up."

A wave washed over Brian's legs from the knees down. He shivered so hard I could see it twenty-five feet away. The wind began to carry snippets of sound to me. "...don't... I don't want..." "...up, you god-damn..." "...please, no..."

Brian turned around and looked in my direction. I couldn't tell if he saw me. If he did, he was smart enough not to let on. Donnie scrambled onto the pier. I wasn't sure what Donnie was doing. He could be planning to kill Brian and then roll his body into the water. But that didn't make sense. If he wanted to frame me, there needed to be a body. The back of the lighthouse might be where he was heading. It didn't look like it could be seen from the parking lot. It was private.

I reached the pier and climbed onto it. Twenty seconds later I got hit with a wave that drenched me from the crotch down. My legs burned with the cold. Brian could see me now, I was sure of it. He was arguing, keeping Donnie's attention. In three quick steps I was directly behind Donnie. I pulled out my Sig and placed it carefully behind his ear.

"Take the gun away from him," I shouted to Brian.

Brian grabbed the Smith & Wesson out of Donnie's hand and let it hang loosely at his side. His breath shaky and coming fast.

"We haven't formally met," I said into Donnie's ear. "I'm Nick Nowak. And you, I think, are Walt Paddington. Or is it Donnie Carr? I'm a little confused."

"I'll give you ten thousand dollars to let me finish this," Donnie hissed. I could barely hear him above the wind.

Brian looked at me for a moment; I couldn't tell if he'd heard Donnie's offer, but he looked concerned.

"I'm not letting you kill anyone while you're wearing my clothes and using my gun. No matter how much money you promise me."

"We can...we can work this out..." Donnie turned to look at me, and I got my first good look at him. His eyes were a warm, friendly brown. He seemed meek, passive almost. His soft face was set in a mask of fear, but that's all it was. A mask. "What are you going to do?"

"We're going to go back to Brian's, and I'm going to call the police." They'll just love this, I thought. Me. Saving a kid. Being a hero. Whoever takes the call, it'll just make their day.

Without warning, Brian lifted the gun and aimed at Donnie.

"No!" I screamed, but he fired anyway. Shooting a gun for the first time isn't as easy as it looks in the movies. The shot went wild, and the recoil knocked Brian on his ass, sending the Smith & Wesson skittering across the concrete. Sprawled on the icy pier, the boy began to slip into the lake.

Instinctively, I pushed Donnie out of the way and got onto my knees, grabbing Brian just before he slid into the water. Relief flooded his face. I stood him up and leaned him against the base of the beacon. Then turned to see that Donnie had gotten hold of the Smith & Wesson and had it aimed right at Brian.

I stepped in front of Brian. I raised my own gun.

"Get out of the way," Donnie told me. His face had lost all warmth. Now he was cold, casually ruthless.

"No," I said, taking a step forward. Donnie took one step back.

"All right," he said blandly. "I'll kill you first."

"You don't want to do that, Donnie." He raised his gun, took aim. "I take extensive notes on all my cases. You kill me and the police will know exactly who you are when they find the notes." It was a lie, but I hoped he'd buy it.

"I know where your office is. I'll stop there on my way out of town."

I took another step toward him. He stepped back. "The notes aren't in my office. They're in my car."

A tremor passed over his face. I was right. He had no idea what kind of car I had. I took advantage of the moment and took another step toward him. He jumped a little and took a final step back, a step that landed him in Lake Michigan.

Brian walked over and stood by me. We watched Donnie struggle in the churning water. He screamed for help once, maybe twice. There was little we could do, even if we'd wanted to. There was no rope nearby. No life preservers. No way for him to get back onto the pier. Even if he'd been able to navigate the waves and get to the pier, it was too icy. He never would have been able to pull himself up.

The current pulled Donnie out into the lake. We were only a hundred feet from the beach. He could have swum it, if the lake had been calm and warm. But it was neither. Briefly, he struggled to keep his head above water. His arms flopped around frantically, then suddenly stopped. Silently, he slipped under the waves.

We waited to see if he'd come back up. He didn't.

I noticed Brian's shivering before my own. We were both soaked in icy water. My jeans were stiff, beginning to freeze. Silently, I led Brian off the pier, and we trudged through the snow, hurrying back to his apartment. We said little on the way.

It seemed to take forever, but we finally got back to his apartment. Once inside, teeth chattering, we pulled off our clothes. "Shower?" I asked.

Brian nodded.

The water stung. Pinpricks covered my entire body. I brushed against Brian. Even under the warm water his skin felt ice cold. I pulled him to me and began to rub some warmth into him.

"Are we going to call the police?" he asked.

I was pretty sure no one saw what happened. Yeah, my gun went into the water with Donnie, but it was unlikely they'd be found anywhere near each other. If they were found at all. Donnie had gone to a lot of trouble to make sure he couldn't be connected to me. I doubted anyone would knock on my door if and when he was found.

Besides, Brian and I hadn't done anything but try to protect ourselves, so we had nothing to worry about. Except, given how fond the Chicago Police Department was of me, they might not see it that way.

"I don't think calling them is a good idea," I said as we got out of the shower.

Brian was visibly relieved. Still, he said, "We just let him die."

"There wasn't anything we could do."

"But we didn't even try." For the first time, I noticed how very blue his eyes were.

"No. We didn't. I'm not going to feel bad about that."

He looked away and then leaned against me. I put my arms around him and held him. Eventually, I leaned over and kissed him. I hadn't expected I'd have sex with him again. I hadn't even wanted to. But there was something about watching a man die together that formed a sort of...connection, I suppose. We'd shared death, and now it made sense to share at least a small sliver of life.

He kissed me back hard, his tongue forcing its way into my mouth. We kissed deeply, until my neck began to ache from bending over. I slid my tongue down his neck and lowered myself to my knees. I found myself at his chest level. I licked his nipples one at a time. He gasped and shivered. But he was no longer cold.

I ran my tongue further down his taut belly and around to his hip. There was a growing bruise there from where he'd fallen on the pier. I kissed it. His cock poked me under the chin. Standing up, I took hold of his prick and led him back to the main room. I pushed him onto the bed and eased myself between his knees. Grabbing hold of his dick, I slipped my tongue between his foreskin and the cock head. I ran it round and round, then pushed the hood back.

Then I dove down, taking his entire dick into my mouth and throat. I bobbed my head up and down on him a half dozen times before I had to come up for air. Brian seemed to need a break, too. He'd begun to squirm and pant. I didn't let the break go on for too long, though. I was back on him. Sucking him, darting my tongue into his piss slit, then pulling him all the way into my throat.

It had been a long while since I'd sucked a dick, and my jaw tired quickly. He didn't seem to mind. As soon as I let his dick fall out of my mouth, his legs went up. I pushed them further into the air and ran my tongue around his hairy pink asshole. It smelled warm and sweet. I rubbed the stubble on my chin across his butt, and he nearly went crazy.

"Oh, God," he moaned. "Just fuck me."

I ignored him and slipped my tongue into his ass. He gasped and clutched at my shoulders. I stopped rimming him and crawled over the bed on top of him. He twisted himself to one side and grabbed a small jar of Vaseline off the nightstand. Opening it, he dipped two fingers in and pulled out a small blob of jelly. Then he reached down and rubbed it all over my dick. He stretched his arm between his legs and lubed his ass, then guided me into him.

I drove into him hard and fast. His legs spread wide, bouncing with each thrust. I grabbed him by the ankles and pushed into him again and again. His mouth fell open, and he pushed his face into the bedspread. I wanted him to look at me, so I slowed almost to a stop. It worked. He turned his head and looked up at me. He reached up and grabbed me by the back of the head. Pulling me close, he kissed me and whispered, "Keep fucking me."

I dipped my prick into him again and again. He held me close. We curled together in a tight ball, kissing and fucking. Then I pulled away from him and gave him a few hard thrusts. His eyes followed me, everything I did, every move I made. He looked right into me, and I could feel it in my chest.

Brian began to masturbate, but I pushed his hand away. I took hold of his dick myself. I didn't jerk it, just held it while I fucked him. His dick quivered each time I pumped him. His eyes opened wider as I teased him. Pumping him hard and fast for a moment or two and then easing off.

Looking down at him in the dim light, the thought flashed across my mind that he could have been Daniel. That he should have been Daniel. That if I'd moved more quickly, recognized the danger earlier, if I'd been able to stop that bat from swinging, we'd have gone home that night. And we would have ended up in a happy, relieved, drunken—

"Please," Brian whispered, pulling me back to the present. "Make me come."

I picked up my pace and started jacking him off. His body went taut, and he let out a long moan as he shot all over his stomach. My own orgasm took me by surprise, and I almost didn't realize I was coming in him until it was nearly over.

I fell on top of him, and he slipped his arms around me. His cum spread over my belly, sticky and warm, as we held each other. When he began to cry softly, I remembered that he was nearly a boy. A boy who'd just learned his mother was dying and whose stepfather had tried to kill him. It must have all come rushing back in on him. Maybe that's what the sex had been for, I thought, to give him a few minutes without death and betrayal. A few minutes of oblivion.

I held him until he stopped crying. "It's been a busy night," I said. "I suppose I should go."

He nodded. When I got out of bed, Brian didn't bother putting any clothes on. He just lay naked on his rumpled sheets, his dick now red and sore-looking as it lazed along his thigh.

I picked up my jeans; they were soaked and freezing cold. There was no way I could slip them back on. I turned around and looked at Brian. "It's okay," he said. "You can stay. There's a dryer in the basement. I'll put some clothes on and take your stuff down."

He didn't move, though. I stood awkwardly in the center of his room, feeling very naked. He seemed like he was warming up to say something. Finally, he did. "What you did for me... I don't know how to thank you."

"Don't worry about it," I told him.

"I'm going to Springfield in the morning. I want to see my mother again, before she...there's an early train. If I give you my phone number down there, will you call me?"

"Sure," I told him. He looked at me like I'd just told him a big lie. And maybe he was right. I had no idea if I'd call him. I sat down on the bed. I could have turned around and cuddled him again. But the mood had shifted.

"There's someone else you're in love with, isn't there?" he guessed.

"No," I lied. "There isn't anyone."

Little Boy Burned

That Valentine's Day I was sleeping alone—by choice.

I was in the middle of a sex dream about the kid in that island movie that came out last year, the one about the boy and girl who get shipwrecked, run around mostly naked, and eventually learn about sex. In my dream, though, there wasn't any girl on the island, and things between the kid and I had begun to get hot and heavy when the phone rang.

"Yeah," I said, untangling my hard-on from my twisted boxers. I glanced at the clock. It was 6:12 a.m. I'd slept a little more than two hours.

"Nick, it's Ross." His voice was electric. "Something's happened. Paradise is on fire."

"I'll be there in a couple of minutes."

I worked the door at Paradise Isle two nights a week and had for a couple of years. Ross was one of the bartenders and my occasional fuck buddy. The nightclub, which we usually called just Paradise, was part of a string of brick storefronts down on Broadway right above Diversey. Ross and I had both finished shifts just hours before.

Groggy and a little horny, I threw on some clothes and ran out to find a cab. It had been easier to find one at three a.m. In the wee hours of a Sunday, cabs cruised around ready to take late-night revelers home. But by six-thirty they'd become scarce. It took almost ten minutes, but I finally got one, and it zipped me down Clark to Diversey. We couldn't make the V turn to get onto Broadway because fire trucks blocked the way. I paid the driver and hopped out.

I got there about six-forty. Smoke was still pouring out of the top of the building, but it looked like the fire was winding down. The sky in the east had turned pink, and I figured the sun would be up in a few minutes. The air was frigid cold, but at least it wasn't snowing. Two big, red fire trucks sat in front of the bar. Hoses crisscrossed the street. Firemen scuttled back and forth; the sidewalk slick with icy water, washing away the dirty snow that currently graced most curbs in Chicago.

I saw our DJ, Miss Minerva Jones, standing on the east side of Broadway in a small crowd. I made my way over. I'd never seen Miss Minerva out of a dress. Usually she favored wrap-around silk disco dresses, six-inch heels, over-teased blond wigs, and a dusting of glitter. That morning, though, she wore a pair of Sergio Valente jeans with their bull's-head logo stitched into the back pockets and a gray parka. She'd left her wig at home and made a half-hearted attempt to take off her makeup. Whiskers were starting to poke their way through the remaining streaks of foundation.

When she saw me, she growled, "Every album I own is in there." In the DJ booth, there were about five milk crates stuffed with the best disco ever recorded. "My life is ruined," she moaned.

"What happened?" I asked.

"No one knows. I was getting ready for bed when I heard the sirens." Miss Minerva had a studio apartment a block away on Clark Street. "They kept getting louder and louder. When they stopped, I knew. I called Davey and then Ross."

I looked around and saw the owner, Davey, and Ross talking with a fireman. Ross was wearing a long, gray wool coat that was actually mine. He'd borrowed it a couple weeks back and now seemed unwilling to return it. Too thin for this weather, the only way I got away with wearing it in winter was to layer up with a corduroy blazer, a flannel shirt, and a T-shirt. Ross wasn't wearing anything underneath but a BVD T-shirt. Even from where I stood, I could see him shivering.

"Bernie was inside," Miss Minerva said flatly. Bernie was another of the bartenders. I didn't know him well. He'd started on the afternoon shift and had only recently begun working the peak nights, Friday and Saturday. I had noticed that, like all of Davey's bartenders, he was a very good-looking boy.

"Is he dead?" I asked.

"No. He's burned pretty bad. They took him to the hospital a few minutes ago." She was sullen, seeming to grind her expensive caps.

"What time did this start?" I asked.

She shrugged. "Not long ago. Close to six?"

"What was Bernie doing here at six in the morning?

"Sleeping in the storeroom," Miss Minerva said. Then with a roll of her eyes she added, "Boyfriend trouble."

I nodded, then headed over to join Davey, Ross, and the fireman. As I walked over, I noticed that an axe had been used to get through the front door where I usually stood checking IDs and keeping an eye out for trouble.

Davey and Ross greeted me, and I patted Davey on the shoulder.

The fireman wore stiff, yellow turnout gear that made him seem enormous. His face was smudged with soot, and he smelled like sweet, acrid smoke. He explained, "It appears the fire began near the bar or possibly even behind it. Accelerants were used, but it could have been bottles of liquor."

"151 Rum would have done it," said Ross.

"It's arson," the fireman said bluntly.

Davey went pale. "Someone did this on purpose?"

"We're not finding any signs of forced entry."

"What does that mean?" Davey asked.

"It could mean a lot of things," I interrupted. Davey didn't seem to understand the situation, but I did, and I didn't think he should say anything else. The fireman gave me a look. His eyes were a sharp blue. We stared each other down for a moment. And then he said, "I'll be back to talk to you later." He walked away.

Davey shook his head, confused. Paradise was his world. It was the second bar he'd put together. The first had been called The Cellar and had a five-year run in Old

Town. He'd hit at just the right time. Disco was big then, and there had been long lines around the block on Fridays and Saturdays. Paradise Isle was successful, but not on the same scale.

Ross pulled out a pack of Camel Lights. He offered me one, and I took it. We lit up and smoked for a minute. "If there are no signs of forced entry, it means that whoever started the fire was let in or had a key," I explained.

"They had a key?" Davey wondered. "How would they get a key?"

"They might have hidden somewhere," suggested Ross. "In the bathroom maybe?"

I took a drag on my cigarette and said, "The thing is, Davey, you're gonna be the most likely suspect."

He blushed a little. "I have an alibi." Davey had a much younger, Asian boyfriend who barely spoke English and called the bar if Davey was five minutes late leaving.

"Doesn't matter," I said. "You could have hired someone to start the fire."

"I love this place. I would never burn it down."

"You have insurance, right?"

He nodded.

"That's your motive."

"What, they think I burned the place down so I could redecorate?"

I smiled. "That's a better reason than some I've heard."

"I have to go to the hospital and see how Bernie's doing," Davey said, as though to himself. He walked away without saying goodbye. Then he turned and came back.

"Find out," he said. "Find out who did this."

# # #

I could have told Davey this wasn't exactly the kind of case I took. As a private investigator, I handled mostly background checks, a little security, and the occasional skip trace. I'd never done an arson investigation, even when I was on patrol. Sure, in the six years I spent on the job with the Chicago PD, I'd worked some fires, but only around the edges—crowd control and canvassing neighborhoods. I'd never been the actual investigator.

Still, Davey was in trouble, and I couldn't turn him down.

Ross and I walked up to The Melrose and had some breakfast. The Sunday morning breakfast rush had just begun. The crowd reflected the neighborhood and was a mix of preppies, who worked downtown in the financial district, and queers, who worked wherever they could. The thing they had in common was sleeping late on Sunday mornings, picking up the *Sunday Herald,* and chowing down on eggs Benedict.

We slipped into a red vinyl booth and asked for coffee. It took a while, but when it finally came, Ross asked me, "What should we do first?"

I ignored the question—particularly the 'we' part—and instead asked, "How was your Valentine's Day?"

"We worked, remember?"

"After that." Ross had a boyfriend named Earl Silver who wrote a gossip column, called "The Silver Spoon," for the *Daily Herald* and had a wife and kids in Naperville. He'd shown up at Paradise just after midnight and waited until Ross got off at two a.m.

"It was okay. Nice, I guess." He studied me for a moment, "You're not jealous, are you?"

"Of course I am," I joked. "I've always had a thing for Earl."

"Right," Ross said, then asked his question again. "So, what are we going to do first?"

I considered for a moment. It wasn't my style to work with a partner, but I had no intention of sending Davey a bill and a lot needed doing. Part of me didn't want Ross around while I investigated this, but the offer was too good to pass up.

"We need to knock on doors and see if anyone saw anything. We should try to get started around eight-thirty, before people start their day."

Ross nodded. "What should I ask?"

"Basically, if they saw anything. And if they did, find out exactly what they saw. You could also ask if they've seen anything suspicious in the last week or so, especially at night."

"Got it," said Ross. "So...who do you think did it?"

"No idea. What kind of enemies does Davey have?" Though we'd both known Davey the same amount of time, Ross worked shifts during the week when business was slower and the staff had more downtime. He was more likely to see or hear things than I was.

"Everyone loves Davey," he said.

"Fire inspector been in recently?"

"I don't know. Maybe." Ross looked at me funny. "You don't think someone in the fire department..."

"Probably not. Davey's been in the business a long time. He knows who to pay off. Still, it was worth asking."

"You have to bribe people?" Ross came from a town downstate aptly named Normal.

"It's Chicago. If you don't make the right payoffs, they write you up and fine you until you do. I suppose if you're really stubborn they might burn you out." I shrugged.

A waitress came by and took our order. I had a ribeye steak with eggs, while Ross ordered a Belgian waffle with strawberries. I chuckled to myself. Waffles were a kid's breakfast, and Ross reminds me of a big kid. He's a boy-man. Freckles and a cowlick over his left eye, and he has arms that are so muscular, he could crack open a walnut in the crook of his elbow.

When the waitress left, I asked, "You see any Outfit types coming in?"

"Outfit?"

"Yeah, like mafia."

"I really am a hick, aren't I?" Ross said. He thought about it for a moment. "Every so often there's someone who stands out. Middle-aged guys who look kind of straight. But I don't remember anyone who looked, you know, criminal."

Bars like Paradise had been subject to various kinds of extortion by the Outfit for decades. If Davey had objected, refused, or even attempted to negotiate, he could have made himself a target for retaliation by The Outfit. For that matter, the Chicago PD has been known to operate in exactly the same way, though since they couldn't raid bars anymore they'd lost a lot of their leverage. "I'll talk to Davey about that," I said.

When our breakfasts arrived, we split up the neighborhood between bites. I took a fifteen-story building across from Paradise called The Shore. Shaped in a wide U, the building looked to have about a hundred apartments in it. Of course, I'd focus on the west side, which faced Broadway. Ross would take the smaller two- and three-story buildings up and down Broadway and check out a couple apartment buildings on Clark behind the bar. We agreed to meet in the lobby of The Shore when we finished.

"Do you think we'll run into any cops doing the same thing?" Ross asked.

"I doubt it," I said. I didn't think anyone on the arson squad would think it worth interrupting their Sunday for a fire in a gay club. They'd start nosing around tomorrow, unless something more important turned up.

We paid our tab and walked back down to Paradise. Chicago is made up of dozens of neighborhoods, most of which have fuzzy, ill-defined boundaries. Paradise Isle was located in a part of town that some people called Lincoln Park and others referred to as New Town. Generally, the distinction was based on the income bracket you wanted to project. If you cared whether people thought you had money or not, then you called it Lincoln Park. If you didn't give a crap, you said New Town.

The sky had turned a brilliant blue, and the sun had melted the last of the snow, but the wind was bitter cold, and Ross' cheeks glowed cherry red. He still wore my wool overcoat, while I had on a hip-length, sheepskin jacket lined with fleece that I'd bought while I was still at the Training Academy. I was nice and toasty, while Ross was freezing his ass off. I wanted to put my arm around him, get him warmed up. But it wasn't the kind of thing you did on the streets of Chicago. Not unless you wanted to deal with catcalls and assholes jumping you. I kept my arm to myself.

When we got in front of The Shore, with its yellow brick and sculpted cement embellishments, I said "see you later" to Ross and went into the glass lobby. The lobby had been added for security sometime in the seventies and clashed with the much older, more elegant architecture of the rest of the building. I walked over to the buzzer system, which had one buzzer for each apartment lined up in four rows of about twenty-five each. I ran my hand up and down one of the rows until someone buzzed the security door and let me in.

This type of canvass was a lot of what I'd done as a beat cop. Whenever someone got robbed, beaten, or killed, beat cops would start things off by securing the crime scene and keeping witnesses in place. When the detectives showed up, they'd stand around the crime scene coming up with ideas, one of which was always to send the beat cops out to canvass. It was a little like being a door-to-door salesman. Except you weren't selling anything, so it was a harder for people to hate you. Not that they didn't hate you anyway. Sometimes just interrupting a person's day is enough to get them to condemn you to hell or insult your mother. Canvassing took patience.

Starting on the west side of the first floor, I was able to talk to three of the tenants in the four apartments that faced Broadway. None of them heard or saw anything before the fire trucks arrived. Still, I took out my pad for each person and took down a couple notes. Mostly notes like "apartment 106 saw nothing, heard nothing." I left a business card with each of them.

It was the same deal on floors two, three, and four, except that there were fewer people home. On the fifth floor, I got lucky. In apartment 504, an elderly woman named Ruthie Carter opened the door and smiled at me. Wearing a thin housecoat and a rusty orange cardigan she'd probably knitted herself, she was hunched over by time and had to turn to one side to peek up at me. Her face was deeply creased.

"Good morning, ma'am. I'm Nick Nowak. I'm a private investigator looking into the fire across the street."

"Private investigator? You mean like *Magnum, PI*?" She asked. Her voice was crisp and sharp.

"I'm not sure what that is, ma'am."

"You're not sure? Why, it's a TV show. It's on Thursday nights at eight o'clock. Don't you watch TV?" Her tone suggested she considered television viewing as necessary as breathing.

"I don't have a television," I explained. It had moved out with Daniel, and I'd never bothered to replace it.

"What on earth do you do without a TV?"

"I do a lot of things. Can you tell me if you happened to see or hear anything unusual last night? Between five and five-thirty?"

"Why don't you come in," she invited me, and then hobbled away from the front door. It was a studio apartment. In one corner sat a nicely made double bed, in another a recliner with a television balanced on a small table a few feet in front of it. I followed the woman over to a small dining table in front of the window. She sat and looked out. She had an excellent view of Paradise Isle.

"Hawaii," she said abruptly. My stomach sank. I worried she might be half crazy.

"What about Hawaii, ma'am?"

"That's where Magnum, PI lives. It looks pretty on TV, but I could never leave Chicago. I've been here seventy-four years."

"Did you happen to see anything this morning?"

She nodded. "I have the insomnia."

"So you're up at night a lot of the time."

"Oh, it's terrible. If I get two good hours of sleep, well, I consider myself lucky. Very lucky."

I took a seat across from her. "And this morning you were sitting right here looking out the window."

"Yes, I was."

"What did you see?"

She lowered her voice to a whisper. "You know that's where the fancy boys go, don't you?"

"Yes, ma'am." I knew she'd tell me eventually; I just wasn't sure I had the patience to wait.

"He ran out of there around five-thirty."

"Who did?"

She shrugged. "I don't know. I don't know any fancy boys."

"Tell me what he looked like."

"He wasn't fat. And he wasn't short." Ruthie would exasperate the police when they showed up. The thought made me want to giggle.

"Was he white? Or black?"

She thought about it. "White. I'm pretty sure. He was wearing a hat. And one of those balloon coats."

"A down coat," I suggested.

"A what?"

"A coat full of feathers. Like a pillow."

"It sure looked like a pillow."

"Was he young or old?"

She thought about it. "Couldn't have been old. He was running. I haven't run like that in forty years."

"Did you see where he went?"

She nodded solemnly. I waited. "He came into The Shore."

I looked out the window. It faced Broadway. The entrance to The Shore was on Surf. There wasn't any way she could have seen him enter the building. I decided not to contradict her. The rest of the information seemed good, what there was of it. I listened to two stories about her daughter who never visited, then said my goodbyes, making sure to give her my card in case she remembered anything else.

On the next few floors, people either weren't home or had slept well all night long. Which didn't stop them from wanting to tell me who they suspected, which was usually the Commies or the colored. When I got to the fourteenth floor, I got lucky again—although in a completely different way.

It was 1407, all the way in the back. I didn't think you could see much this far up, so I was almost ready to call it quits. The guy who answered the door was close to twenty, about five foot six, stood in the doorway wearing nothing but a pair of white bikini briefs, and had a set of abs that looked more like armor than muscles.

"My name is Hector," he said before I'd even had a chance to introduce myself. He had a slight Spanish accent.

I told him who I was and what I was doing. He didn't seem to pay much attention. "Come in, please. And could you close the door?"

I'm thirty-two years old, stand six foot three, and weigh two-ten dripping wet. My hair is brown, my eyes are green, and I wear a mustache. I guess you could say I have a kind of brooding good looks; strangers have been known to stop and tell me to smile. There's a certain kind of guy who takes one look at me and that's it, they're hooked. I don't quite understand it, but I rarely object. From the way Hector waddled across the room, giving me a good look at his well-formed buttocks, I figured he was one of those guys.

There wasn't anything in the apartment but a brown leather sofa with about a hundred tufts and an orange and red Chinese rug spread in front of it. Hector curled up on the sofa and said, "I've been expecting you."

"You have?" I asked.

"Yes. My psychic told me a tall, tall man would come into my life, and he would give me a present. Did you bring me a present?"

I almost laughed, but was too taken by his tight, muscular body and the dimples that appeared in his cheeks when he smiled. His dark brown eyes weren't too bad, either. "I think your psychic must have someone else in mind."

"Maybe. Or maybe you'll bring me a present later?" He smiled again. I tried not to smile back.

I took a look out Hector's window. He couldn't have seen anything helpful. Not from this height and not from this angle. I decided it would be a good idea to get out of there.

"Well, thank you, I think I should be heading out."

"Don't you want to know who burned down Paradise?"

I braced myself. He might be Cuban and about to tell me that Fidel Castro did it. "Sure, who burned it down?"

"The Surfside Neighborhood Association."

Well, at least that was a new answer. "Okay, tell me about it."

He frowned. "Not if you're just going to stand there. Sit down."

I sat on the far end of the sofa. He slid himself over to me. He wore lemony cologne that made him smell fresh and appetizing.

"What makes you think the neighborhood association burned down the bar?"

"It makes much sense. They hate the bar. They say it is noisy and interrupts the parking in the neighborhood and it brings a bad element right into their backyard. Are you a bad element? I'm a bad element."

"Where did you hear this? Do you go to their meetings?"

"Oh no! I would not go to their stupid meetings. They made a sheet...a, how do you say...an announcing. That's wrong. Announce-ment." He jumped up and ran to his small kitchen. Rifling through the drawers, it took him a moment to come up with a single sheet of paper. "Here it is. They put one under all doors."

He handed me a sheet of paper, then sat down next to me. Somehow he managed to get even closer. I tried to focus on the flyer. It was handwritten and then Xeroxed onto marigold-colored paper. It announced the time of a Surfside Neighborhood Association meeting that would take place in a few days. The subject was Paradise Isle and the bad element it brought into the backyard of decent, hardworking families. At the bottom of the sheet it offered more information by contacting John Bradford. It gave his phone number as well as his apartment number, 304. I hadn't spoken to him. His had been one of the apartments where no one answered.

"Can I keep this?" I asked Hector.

"Yes, you can," he said. Then he gasped, "Maybe she was wrong. Maybe you will not give me a present. Maybe I will give you one."

It took me a moment, then I realized that he was calling the flyer his present. I folded it and put it in my jacket pocket. "Maybe," I said.

Hector eyed me a moment, then slipped out of his bikini briefs. His cock was fat and uncut. Semi-hard, it called a lot of attention to itself lolling there on his hip. "You want to fuck me?" he asked.

"The thought crossed my mind," I replied honestly.

Hector got up and left the room. Seconds later he was back with a bottle of lotion in one hand. In the middle of the empty rug, he got down on his hands and knees. He spread some lotion on his ass and some more on his dick. He looked over at me and said, "I'm ready."

Generally, I like a little foreplay. But there was something about the business-like way he approached the whole thing, not to mention the way his ass curved up into the air, that had me ready to go.

I walked over and stood behind him. Unzipping my jeans, I lowered them to my ankles. Then I dropped my boxers. Hector looked over his shoulder and took a look at my swelling prick. He lisped something in Spanish that sounded like, "Eye deoth meoth." I didn't have a clue what he meant, and didn't care.

Getting on my knees behind him, I edged forward until the tip of my cock tickled his wet pucker hole. Holding myself at the base, I slapped my hard dick against Hector's nice fat ass a couple times. I put my hands on his hips and pulled him back onto me. A moan escaped from his lips, like air being let out of a balloon. He continued to mumble in Spanish. I assumed it had something to do with the way I was pumping his ass. I closed my eyes and fucked him for a good long time. My thighs slapped into his ass over and over, making a clapping noise that echoed in the nearly empty room.

With his warmth surrounding me, I could feel his racing pulse beating on the base of my dick each time I paused to catch my breath. I wondered if our hearts were going to match each other. But then I stopped thinking altogether and just fucked.

His Spanish got more intense, and I figured that meant he was about to come. I picked up my speed and fucked him all the harder. He rewarded me by clamping down his sphincter muscle while he came. It took another few minutes, but I kept fucking him until I came myself. It felt like untying a knot deep inside me.

When I stood to pull up my pants, I noticed I had a couple of angry red rug burns on my knees. Hector stood up, cupping one hand in front of him. I realized then that he'd carefully come into his own hand. I wondered if what he'd been saying all along in Spanish was, "Don't come on my rug."

Hector went to wash up. I zipped my pants and realized I'd never taken off my sheepskin jacket. I was sweating, so I went ahead and took it off. That left me in a button-down shirt with my shoulder holster holding my 9mm Sig Sauer firmly under my arm. When Hector came back into the room, he eyed my gun. "I'm glad you did not show me that before. I would come very fast."

I smiled. "Is there anything else you can think of that might help? With my investigation?"

"No, I think I say everything." The way he bit his lip told me he had more he wanted to say.

"What?" I asked.

He shrugged. "I go to Paradise Isle every once in a while. I remember you standing at the door. You don't remember me, do you?"

"I see a lot of people."

"Still, my feelings are abused."

"Next time I see you, I'll remember you. How about that?" He huffed at the meagerness of my offer. With a nod, I picked up my jacket and walked out of his apartment.

I didn't figure I'd get much out of the people on the fifteenth floor, and I was running late, so I headed for the elevator. The elevator hadn't been updated since the building was built. You opened a door with a handle, then slid a collapsible cage to one side. That allowed you to step into the coffin-like car. It gave a little each time you stepped in. I had the definite feeling it was going to drop fourteen floors.

When I miraculously got out on the first floor, I slipped my jacket back on, heading for the lobby. Ross wore an impatient look on his face. "What took you so long?" he asked the minute he saw me. "I've been waiting almost half an hour."

"It's a big building."

He leaned over, sniffed me, and rolled his eyes. "Nice cologne. Whose is it?"

I hadn't realized, but Hector's fresh and lemony cologne was now all over me. I couldn't help but blush.

# # #

Monday morning, I got the paper to see what they had to say about the fire at Paradise Isle, but they hardly mentioned it. There was a fire on the front page, though. A nightclub in Dublin had burned to the ground, killing forty-some people and injuring hundreds. On scale alone I could see why it was on the front page. Of course, we were local and that should have earned us at least a couple column inches in the lower front corner. But no, the Paradise Isle fire was nowhere near the front page. Toward the back of the front section, I found a two-paragraph blurb that told me even less than I already knew.

Ross had turned up the same flyer I'd gotten from Hector, but not much more. Certainly he hadn't found anyone who'd seen the arsonist in a dark cap and a down coat leaving the building. By this point, I'd begun to doubt whether Ruthie was a valuable witness or not. Thinking she saw the guy go into The Shore when that was impossible lessened her credibility. I wondered how seriously I should take her description.

The night before, Davey had called and asked to meet in front of Paradise in the morning. I keep regular office hours, so ten o'clock Monday morning wasn't a hardship for me. For Ross, it was painful. Used to going to bed at four or five in the morning, he looked something like a junkie on the tail end of a three-day binge.

Davey drove a dusty blue 1976 Cadillac Eldorado that he'd bought when The Cellar was at its peak. He'd parked illegally in front of the burned-out bar and had takeout coffee and donuts spread out on the trunk. Ross was already halfway through his coffee.

"Anyone from the arson squad been here?" I asked as I picked up a Styrofoam cup full of steaming brew.

Davey nodded. "Came around eight. Just left a little while ago."

"They say anything interesting?"

"Just that they've got a suspect."

"That's great," said Ross, a little too enthusiastically. I could tell he wanted to go back to bed. "Who do they think did it?"

"Me," Davey said flatly.

We went silent. I pulled out a box of Marlboro Reds and lit one up. The smoke filled my lungs with a familiar rush; it's stupid, I guess, but a chest full of smoke always makes life seem a little more manageable. "Any word on Bernie?"

With a frown, Davey told us about Bernie. "He's gonna make it. But there are burns on twenty percent of his body. A lot of it's on his face. He's gonna be..." He looked down at the pavement, as though he was looking for something to kick. "He's not gonna be the same."

Under his breath, Ross mumbled, "Ah, shit."

Bernie was only a kid, twenty-two years old, and he had great face. Big crooked smile, creamy cheeks, big brown eyes. His body was okay, but Davey had hired him for his face. Customers left big tips because of his face. Guys chased after that face. It was going to be tough on Bernie figuring out how to get through life without it.

"When can I talk to him?" I asked.

"Soon. He's still pretty doped up. He's not making much sense."

"What do you think happened here, Davey?" I wanted to get him talking first. Direct questions would come later.

"I dunno. I keep going over it in my head. Who would do this to me? I have no idea."

"Have you been greasing the right palms?" I asked.

"My, uh, municipal payments are up to date. I don't think there's a problem there. A bagman comes by once a month for the Outfit. Picks up four hundred bucks."

"And you're current?"

"Yeah, but here's the thing. He's the only one I've ever seen. I don't know where the money goes. I don't even know that it gets where it's going. I never thought that was a problem before, but maybe it is?"

"What's the bagman's name?"

"Mickey Troccoli."

"Mickey?" said Ross. "I know him. I think he hit on me once."

Davey shrugged. Then he looked at me. "Mickey might have started keeping the money, you know? Maybe the Outfit's trying to teach me a lesson I didn't need to learn."

"I'll find out." I was going out on a limb. I still had a few connections, but they didn't always pan out. I wasn't all that sure I *could* find out. "Tell me about The Surfside Neighborhood Association."

"Who?"

Ross pulled out a flyer and handed it to Davey. He looked it over. "Oh, yeah, these jerks. Pain in the ass, that's all."

"You sure?"

"They make a lot of noise, but they can't do anything to me. Like I said, I greased all the right palms." The way he said it made me think that greasing palms was a skill that took years to develop. And it may well have been.

"So, they're frustrated," I speculated.

"Naw, they're do-gooders and church ladies. Not arsonists."

I nodded like I agreed with him, but I didn't. My experience as a cop, not to mention what I've picked up as a PI, told me that anyone was capable of anything. With the right mental gymnastics, a church lady could burn down a gay bar and walk away feeling like she'd just done God's work. I tucked the possibility away for later.

"Can we look around inside?"

Davey looked in both directions and said, "Sure. I don't see why not."

A company had come out and nailed large pieces of plywood to the busted-out front doors. Taped to the wall next to the doors was a Chicago PD sign that told us in very official language not to enter. Ignoring it, Davey opened the door and led us in.

We stood for a moment in the wide foyer where Davey and I set up on Fridays and Saturdays to collect the cover and check IDs. The place smelled smoky, but it was a stale smell, the smell of old, dead smoke. The power was off, so other than the light that came in through the door and a hole the firemen had chopped in the roof, there wasn't a lot of light. Apparently, Davey had gone out and gotten a couple industrial flashlights, because two of them sat there in the foyer. He handed me one.

A lot of the bar is dance floor—expensive dance floor. Thirty feet by thirty feet and made of Plexiglas, the floor lit from the bottom up, and was attached to a fancy light board kept in the DJ booth that controlled the patterns made by colored lights underneath the floor. Now, though, half the dance floor had melted and fallen in on itself.

The tables and chairs that usually sat next to the dance floor had mostly been knocked down, probably by the force of the water hosed onto the fire. One table had the chairs set upside down on top of it. This was one of the side-work duties of the closing bartender. It was done so that a cleaning crew could come in at six o'clock every morning and vacuum the carpet. Sunday morning they'd ended up with the day off.

I made a mental note that Bernie had obviously finished his side work, which suggested he hadn't been interrupted. Nothing prevented him from following his normal routine. Nothing out of the ordinary happened until after four-fifteen or four-thirty.

The booths along the wall seemed relatively undamaged. In keeping with the tropical theme, there were two neon palm trees tacked to the walls. Both of them were destroyed. It was hard to tell if they'd been wrecked by fire or the pressurized water used to put it out. I started taking a good look at the floor. A heavy-duty industrial carpet had been laid through about half the place. The foyer wasn't carpeted. That would be crazy in Chicago—

you'd only get through half a winter before it was ruined. The carpet started about fifteen feet into the club and continued around the dance floor and the table area. It ended at the bar.

Near the bar, most of the stools had fallen over. I moved one of them. Where the stool had lain during the fire, the carpet was untouched. It looked like a weird stencil of the stool. I moved a couple nearby stools and noted the same patterns. But the stools further away didn't have the unburned pattern—they'd been knocked over later.

I walked back over to the chairs near the tables and moved them around. Nothing.

"What are you doing?" Ross asked.

"Three stools at the bar were knocked over either as the fire started or just before. Everything else was knocked over while the fire was being put out."

"What does that mean?" Davey asked.

"I'm not sure. There might have been a struggle. Or the arsonist was angry, throwing things around."

I aimed my flashlight down a hallway to the right of the bar. Off the hallway were several doors: two for the restrooms, one for the office, and one that led up to the DJ booth. I slipped up to the booth first. The darkly tinted window that allowed Miss Minerva to watch the crowd had been busted out. The electronics had been soaked in water and were now useless junk. Miss Minerva's five milk crates full of albums sat by the wall. I leaned over and pulled out an album from the top. It was Sylvester's *Living Proof.* The cardboard casing fell apart in my hands. The record itself might be playable. But without the album covers, Miss Minerva's collection would be scratched and unusable in no time.

I went back downstairs and took a quick tour through the restrooms. Both bathrooms fronted the alley and had windows near the ceiling. The firemen had broken them out. I stood on a waste can in the men's room and tried to inspect the hook on the window. It was broken, but there was no way for me to tell if that had happened before or after a fireman stuck an axe through the window.

The office held even less information. It was a tiny room and had very little smoke or water damage. Squeezed in there were a desk, a filing cabinet, and a safe. The papers on the desk were largely undamaged. That was a good thing for Davey. He'd have all the necessary paperwork he needed to put the place back together.

I went back out to the bar and stood for a minute or so just staring at it. The most severe damage was here. The bar itself was wooden and nearly twenty feet long. I remembered there was some story connected to it. It might have come from The Cellar. I wasn't sure. It wouldn't be going anywhere else, though—except to a landfill somewhere.

It was charred, more so in some places than others. That suggested that there had been several points used to start the fire—if the fire had indeed been started on the bar. But if it hadn't, what would explain the variations? It looked as though someone had taken a bottle of something very flammable—probably alcohol, or several bottles of alcohol—and poured them onto the bar in different spots. While doing this, they may have knocked down a couple stools and not bothered to pick them up. Or someone else had tried to stop them. Either way, they then lit the puddles of liquor.

"What are you looking for?" Ross asked.

"I've never done arson before, but the fireman said it started at the bar. I'm guessing that you look for places where there's a lot of damage."

"You mean the place with the most damage is probably where the fire started?"

"Yes."

He stood next to me, looking at the bar. Davey was wandering around staring at everything. He seemed to be calculating what needed to be redone in order to open again. The bad news that pretty much everything needed to be redone seemed to be sinking in.

"No," Ross said abruptly. "It wouldn't be like that. Not this time." He flipped open the service bar and pulled me behind the bar.

The rubber mat on the floor that prevented the bartenders from slipping on spillage had melted and reformed into a lava-like puddle. Behind the bar, there had been glass shelves in front of a mirror where the liquor was kept. Now, the shelves were shattered and the bottles had burst with the heat of the fire. The mirror was cracked and covered in soot.

Ross pointed at the area where the shelves had been. "The worst damage is back here. This would be the hot spot. But not until the bottles started to blow up."

I looked up at the ceiling. The fire seemed to have spread there quickly, with severe damage above the bar. The hole that had been chopped into the roof was over the dance floor. I asked Ross, "If you were going to burn the place down, how would you do it?"

After thinking about it, he said, "I'd start with the bar. I'd pick out a high-proof liquor and pour it all over the place. I might use a few stacks of cocktail napkins to get things going. But I'd definitely want to be out of here before the bottles started to blow."

I nodded. It confirmed my original thoughts. At the far end of the bar, a door led to the storage room. I walked down and took a look. There was a lot of damage. The walls had burned down to the studs, and the studs were charred. The floor looked dangerously unstable.

The doorway I stood in was the only entrance to the room. That might have been against code, but Davey greased the right palms. Beyond the storeroom, reached via the hallway, were the bathrooms and Davey's small office. Those rooms had windows. The storeroom did not.

A chill went up and down my spine. If Bernie had been sleeping on the boxes in the storeroom when the fire started, he would have been woken when bottles began to explode. He would have had to come through this door. He'd have flung it open to discover the bar engulfed in flames. There wouldn't have been any option but to run through the flames. Bernie couldn't have stayed in the storeroom, not with all the liquor in there ready to explode. It would have been suicide.

I imagined him running through the flames, scrambling to get over the bar, knocking down barstools, rolling around on the carpet trying to put himself out. It was a terrible thought.

When I'd seen enough, we went back outside. Davey thanked us for coming, then climbed into the Eldorado and drove off. I turned to Ross and said, "I've got some things I need to do. I'll give you a call later on."

"Why can't I come with you?"

"Because we're not *McMillan and Wife*."

He frowned. I could tell he was angry.

"You can't come with me for this. It's a family thing."

# # #

I grew up in the Chicago neighborhood called Bridgeport. Lots of Irish, Lithuanians, and Poles live there. It's sort of a citified version of *Leave It to Beaver* Land. Yeah, if you scratch the surface things are completely screwed up, but what's important is that it makes a pretty picture. A lot of cops and other city employees live in Bridgeport, and up until two years ago every mayor since 1933. Bridgeport's two big claims to fame are Comiskey Park and the fact that it's one of the very, very few white neighborhoods left on the Southside.

Most of my family is in the Chicago Police Department. Up until a couple years ago, so was I. Then my ex-lover Daniel and I got into an altercation with some suburban kids outside a gay bar. We got bashed. Daniel ended up with a badly injured eye. I ended up losing my boyfriend, my job, and my family. I'm not trying to whine. It's just what happened.

Approaching anyone in my family is unpleasant. Every once in a while I run into someone, usually in their official capacity, and it's not exactly a tea party. In order to trace the payments that Davey made to the Outfit, I had to track down my uncle, Sergeant Jack Nowak. Jack is short for Jacek, but if you call him that he'll have you in a headlock before you've stopped talking.

In a police department dominated by Irish cops, my Polack family doesn't do so well. My Uncle Jack was one of the few who made it to sergeant. To do it, he had to get himself pretty dirty. In fact, he was probably the dirtiest cop I knew. I figured the pension he expected from the Outfit was going to put the pension from the CPD to shame. He had about two years left until retirement, and from what I heard he'd been doing what he could to squeeze every last bit of graft out of those two years. Occasionally he does a bit of police work, but most of the time he holds court at a diner on 31st near McGuane Park.

I wandered around my neighborhood until I found my baby-blue Plymouth Duster and, after a half dozen tries, managed to get it started. I zig-zagged my way over to the Kennedy and stayed on it until it became the Dan Ryan and took me into Bridgeport. I got off the freeway and took a quick detour to the house I grew up in.

A one-story, brick bungalow, it had two bedrooms, a fireplace in the living room, and a formal dining room. My father retired from the department a year or so ago, and I'd heard through the grapevine that he and my mother had bought a mobile home in Phoenix for the winters. It seemed like this might actually be true, because when I unlocked the front door and walked in, the house was cold and smelled of dust. I headed to the breakfront in the dining room and grabbed what I'd come for. I was in and out in less than sixty seconds. Still, my heart beat like I'd spent the whole morning breaking and entering. Back in the Duster, it took another ten minutes to get to 31st and another ten minutes to find a parking space.

The diner was called Molly's, and I remembered going there with my family when I was a boy. Each table had its own private jukebox stuck to the wall, and I remember flipping through and begging my father for a quarter so I could play three songs. I walked in and noted that, in twenty years, little had changed. Not much had been cleaned, either.

My uncle Jack sat in a booth at the back, near the restrooms and the payphone. He was just past fifty and spreading around the middle. He hadn't bothered to buy a larger uniform, so there was a constant struggle between the buttons on his shirt and his belly. I slipped into the booth across from him.

"Hello, Uncle Jack." He was my father's baby brother. Spoiled as a child and spoiled as an adult.

"Well, if it isn't the family fag."

"Nice to see you, too."

The waitress started to come over, but he waved her off. "He ain't staying." Then he stared me down. He took a leisurely sip of his coffee and said, "What do you want? I'm busy."

"A bar called Paradise Isle burned down. I'm looking into it."

"I heard about that." He shrugged. "Sounds like someone did the community a service."

Keeping my voice even, I said, "The bar belongs to a friend of mine. Another friend of mine got pretty badly hurt."

He gave me a blank look, then said, "And?"

"A bagman comes by once a month, picks up a donation. Guy's name is Mickey Troccoli. I need to know who he works for."

Uncle Jack laughed. "What do you wanna know that for?"

"I need to make sure the money got where it was supposed to. I need to make sure there hasn't been a misunderstanding."

"Why the fuck should I help you?"

"Because we're family."

He broke out in a big laugh. "Because we're family? Shit, that's a reason to shoot you in the back of the head and dump you in the Chicago River."

I sat very still for a few seconds, then said, "Because I still have a key to my parents' house."

He glared at me.

"I stopped by this morning and picked up the family photo albums." I let it sink in. My parents had been very social in the sixties and seventies. They had a lot of backyard barbecues, clambakes, and Christmas parties. The albums were full of pictures of cops: some of them okay guys, a lot of them crooked. Some of the pictures included the people they were crooked with.

"That don't mean shit," he said.

"Not by itself, no. I don't even know who all the people are in the pictures. But there's a guy at the *Daily Herald*, he might know. I figure if I go down and tell him every rumor I ever heard about you, one or two of them might have to do with people in the pictures. That'll make a nice article with pretty pictures, don't you think?"

He stared at me a long time, then he smiled. "What the fuck...it's no skin off my nose. Mickey Troccoli works for Jimmy English."

"How do I get to see Jimmy English?"

"I make a phone call." Uncle Jack squeezed himself out of the booth. He walked over to the payphone, dropped in a dime and dialed. He turned away from me as he talked. A minute later, he hung up and came back to the table.

He gave me Jimmy English's address and said, "He's expecting you."

I thought about saying thank you, but that seems kind of wrong after you blackmail someone, so I just nodded. I got up, but before I walked away I told my uncle, "By the way, I'm gonna take those pictures and give them to my lawyer, along with some notes on the things I remember. Just in case you have any ideas about dumping me in the Chicago River."

I didn't think he was serious about killing me and tossing me in the river. But you don't want to be wrong about a thing like that.

"You're a pain in the ass," he told me.

Driving out to Oak Park, I couldn't help but think about how my ex Daniel would have handled the conversation with Uncle Jack. He'd have gone ballistic when Uncle Jack made the community service crack. He'd have called him a bigot or an Archie Bunker or some other completely accurate name.

It wouldn't have helped one bit. Not really. In fact, it would have gotten him thrown out of there pretty damn fast. Still, part of me wished I could be like that. Part of me wanted to scream in people's faces when they pulled that shit. There was some satisfaction in blackmailing my uncle, but not a lot. Blackmail was a crime. It was dirty. It made me as bad as my Uncle Jack.

As the neighborhoods improved, so did my mood. Oak Park is a well-manicured suburb for the well-to-do. It's old money, family money. Nothing nouveau like you might find in Naperville. People here didn't talk about where their money came from. That was impolite, largely because few of them had actually earned it.

Jimmy English lived in a two-story, brick colonial. A brand-new, black Sedan DeVille sat in the driveway. Even though the weather had been crappy, with the occasional light snow that turned into dirty slush within minutes, the car was spotless. It gleamed like it was still on the showroom floor.

I parked across the street and walked up to the front door. Rang the bell. A few moments later, a small European woman in a maid's uniform opened the door. I told her my name and that Jimmy was expecting me. In heavily accented English, she told me I should follow her.

The place was like a museum. Everything carefully displayed and lovingly tended. I couldn't tell what the museum honored other than good taste and upper middle class splendor. The maid led me into the kitchen and then down the stairs into the basement.

The basement had been finished in thickly varnished, knotty pine. The varnish was old and turned the wood a jaundiced yellow. At the far end sat a bar with red leather stools. Standing behind the bar was an elderly man in a white shirt and gray slacks. The slacks were held halfway up his stomach by a pair of suspenders.

Without introducing me, the maid turned and went back upstairs. I took a seat at the bar and said, "Are you Jimmy English?"

He nodded and asked me what I'd have to drink. It was around two o'clock in the afternoon. A little early for me to start throwing them back, but Jimmy English didn't seem the kind of guy you said "no" to unless you absolutely had to.

I asked for a scotch, and he seemed disappointed. "You don't want anything more complicated?"

"Sure. I'll have a Rusty Nail." With just two ingredients, it wasn't much more complicated than scotch on the rocks, but Jimmy happily searched his copy of Mr. Boston's for the recipe.

"I'm learning to be a bartender," he said while he flipped pages. I hadn't noticed before, but his bar, unlike the bars in other suburban homes, was professionally set up. He had every kind of liquor you could ask for and all the gadgets professionals use. The only thing missing was a cash register.

"You know, that's funny," I said, trying to keep the nervousness out of my voice. "Because I'm here about a bar."

"Yes, I know." He found the drink recipe and frowned a little when he saw how easy it was. I'm sure he was hoping I'd order something tricky like a Pink Lady or Grasshopper. He set about making my drink anyway.

"Do you mind if I smoke?" I asked.

"No, not at all." He slid an ashtray in front of me; inside it was a pack of matches that had a nicely designed logo on the front: Jimmy's Place.

I lit my cigarette while Jimmy filled a glass with ice, poured in some top-shelf scotch, and followed it with a shot of Drambuie. He stuck a swizzle stick in the glass, placed a napkin in front of me, and set my drink down. He stood back, pleased with himself.

"Should I leave you a tip?"

He broke out laughing. I took a drag off my cigarette and waited for him to finish. For some reason he seemed to like me. I couldn't think why, but supposed it didn't matter. "You think I burned down the sissy bar, don't you?" he said.

"I don't think anything yet. Right now I'm asking questions." He nodded. "Guy named Mickey Troccoli comes by every month and my friend gives him a bag of cash. Does it get where it needs to go?"

"Why don't you ask Mickey?"

"Because if the money's not getting where it needs to, he's not going to tell me." Jimmy knew that, of course; he just wanted to make sure I wasn't an idiot.

"I have no reason to burn down your friend's bar," he said simply. Implying that if he'd had a reason, he would have gone right ahead and done it.

"Do you have any idea who did?"

He shook his head. "But you'll find out, won't you?"

I stood up, putting out my cigarette, and said, "I intend to, yes."

"Sit down. Finish your drink."

I didn't want to. I wasn't exactly sure how high up in the Outfit Jimmy was, but he was high enough to scare the shit out of me. I sat down and took a big gulp of my Rusty Nail.

"You used to be a policeman like your uncle," he said, as though it was idle chit-chat.

"I used to be a policeman, but, no, not like my uncle."

Jimmy smiled. "From time to time I have odd jobs I need taken care of."

"I just said I'm not like my uncle."

"I heard you." His voice was calm, casual. That made it even more frightening. "I like that you came here. That took courage. You needed to find out something for your friend, and you didn't let anything stop you. That's good." I managed to get down the rest of my drink. He glanced at it and continued. "Sometimes I need men like your uncle. Less often, I need men like you."

"Are you asking for my business card?"

"I don't need it. If I want you, I'll find you."

# # #

When I got back to my neighborhood, it took nearly a half hour to find a parking place. The temperature had risen to about forty while I was in the suburbs, a fluke warm day in the middle of a crap winter. The weatherman was predicting rain in the early evening, followed by freezing during the middle of the night. Not the kind of conditions that encourage people to run out in their cars. I finally found a spot above Addison on Fremont and walked the four blocks to my apartment.

I live in the basement of a two-story, brown brick apartment building on Roscoe near Halsted. I'm not sure what my apartment was originally meant to be, but I know it wasn't an apartment. In the summer, the place is nicely landscaped, and I get to look out at flowers through my street-level windows. In the winter, snow piles up against those windows, and I can pretend I live in an igloo.

When I walked into my building's small foyer, I immediately saw Brian Peerson leaning up against my door with a bag of groceries at his feet. "What's up?" I asked.

"I brought dinner. I thought we could have like a Valentine's thing. You know, since you had to work on the real Valentine's Day." I could tell he was itching to add, "and because you didn't call me yesterday."

"Come on in," I said. I'd met Brian about a month before and sort of saved his life from a murderously inclined stepfather. We'd been seeing each other a little since he got back from burying his mother downstate. So far, it hadn't worked out too badly for me, but I suspected that wasn't the case for Brian.

My apartment is like a maze. The kind of place where a hamster might feel right at home. Four rooms that curl around each other. A living room, a bedroom, a kitchen, and a junk room. There's a bathroom with a claw-footed bathtub and a couple of oddly-shaped closets. The radiators hang from the ceiling and hiss at my guests— even if I like them.

When we worked our way around to the kitchen, Brian unpacked the groceries. "Did you have a nice Valentine's Day?"

"Not really. I worked 'til one a.m. And then the place I work burned down."

He turned and studied my face to see if I was joking. "It really burned down?"

"Yes. I've been trying to find out what happened."

"Oh," he said.

Obviously, he'd been angry I hadn't called him. But now that I had a good excuse, he relaxed a little. Of course, I probably wouldn't have called him anyway.

"I'm going to make spaghetti with meat sauce. Nothing fancy."

"Sounds great," I said. Actually, the whole idea was pissing me off. I kept that to myself, though, since if I said anything, he'd ask me why it pissed me off. I didn't know, and I didn't much care to figure it out.

On my counter, Brian laid out a large can of sauce imported from Italy, a box of thin spaghetti, a triangle of Parmesan cheese, fresh vegetables, a half-pound of ground sirloin, a loaf of Italian bread, and a jug of red wine. "I went to Treasure Island." The meal was going to be a lot fancier than anything I made myself. I'd only been in Treasure Island once. I didn't recognize half the things they sold, so I left.

I sat down at the table and lit a cigarette. I watched as Brian opened the bottle of wine and poured me a glass. He sliced up an onion and a green pepper. Without asking, he dug around my cupboards until he found a frying pan. After glancing at it, he put it in the sink and re-washed it. While he did this, he talked about his mother. She'd died of cancer a few weeks before. The recipe was hers; he hoped it came out as good as it did when she made it.

He was a good-looking kid. He was twenty-one, about five seven, dirty blond with blue eyes and a broad, toothy smile he hadn't had much opportunity to use around me. As he walked back and forth in the small kitchen, I couldn't help but watch his ass. It filled out his jeans in an impressive way. I wished I could like him more than I did.

His falling for me was understandable, I guess. I'd saved his life. That brings up a lot of feelings, feelings he mistook for love. I wasn't in love with him. But if I had to, I'd save his life again. Not that it counts for much when a guy looks at you like you're his future.

I was starting a second glass of wine when the doorbell rang. I walked down the hall to the living room, through the junk room and down another hall until I got to the front. I opened the door and there was Ross shivering in my wool coat. The promised rain had started and it looked like it was coming down cold.

"I want to know what you found out," Ross said.

"When are you going to give me back my coat?" I asked.

"Never."

I fake-frowned at him and said, "Come on in."

He stomped his wet shoes by the door, and I told him to go ahead and take them off. Quickly, he stepped out of them and then peeled off my coat. Underneath he wore a pair of Calvin Klein jeans and a thermal T-shirt that had been dyed lime green. He grabbed me and kissed me, hard with a lot of tongue. I kissed him back and then broke away.

"Brian's here. He's making dinner."

"Oh, you want me to go?"

"No. Stick around."

I led Ross into the kitchen and introduced him to Brian. Brian gave Ross a firm handshake.

"There's enough food for Ross to stay for dinner, isn't there?"

When Brian hesitated, Ross stepped in and said, "I don't have to stay, it's okay."

"Don't be silly," I said. I turned to Brian and said, "He just lost his job. He could use a free meal."

"Sure, there's plenty," Brian said.

"Davey said my job would be there when they reopen."

"Which isn't going to happen for at least six months," I pointed out.

"They might need an extra waiter at the French Bakery." Brian worked at a restaurant in the Loop. Although why he was still there, I didn't understand. I didn't know exactly how much money he'd just inherited, but it was enough that his stepfather had tried to kill him. He obviously didn't need to work as a waiter.

I poured Ross a glass of wine and refilled Brian's glass. Brian kept cooking while I caught Ross up on the day's events. When I started talking about Jimmy English, Brian interrupted and asked, "You really had a meeting with a mafia guy?"

"Yeah, I did."

"Were you scared?"

"No," I lied.

The look Brian gave me made me glad I wasn't going to fall in love with him. He was the kind of guy who'd eventually ask me to stop doing what I do, and I'd have to tell him no.

"So, it's definitely not the Outfit," said Ross.

I shook my head.

"We need to talk to John Bradford," Ross said. I could tell he was getting into this. Too into it.

"He the guy on the flyer?" I asked.

"Yeah," said Ross. "There's no telling how many crazies he's got in his group."

"It's a possibility," I said. "When's their meeting?"

"Tomorrow night."

Maybe I should go, I wondered. Then I said, "Mostly I need to talk to Bernie, see if he heard or saw anything."

We wondered how bad Bernie's injuries might actually be. Worried about how well Davey was going to recover from this, and then dinner was ready. The three of us squeezed around my tiny kitchen table and ate. The radiator on the ceiling popped on, and between that and the wine the atmosphere was warm and homey. Brian had done a good job. The meal was perfect. Whether it was the food or the wine, his mood brightened and he got friendlier. Even to the point that he started to laugh whenever Ross made a joke.

After we were finished, I got an idea about how I wanted the rest of the evening to go. I went into the bathroom and shut the door. Reaching under the sink, I felt around until I found a paper packet I'd taped up underneath. I pulled it off the cast iron sink and unfolded it. Inside were three Quaaludes.

I walked back to the kitchen and set a pill in front of each of us. "Dessert," I said.

"What is it?" Brian asked.

"It's a 'lude."

"Sex is great on 'ludes," Ross added. The implications were clear. Brian looked at me and then at Ross. He frowned a little, but he picked up the round white pill, swallowing it with a gulp of his wine. Ross and I followed suit.

We sipped wine for a few more minutes without saying much, then I stood up and said, "Follow me, boys." I led them into my bedroom. I didn't have much in there except a mattress on the floor and an old, beat-up bureau.

Standing near the mattress, I pulled them both toward me. I kissed Brian while I ran my hand over Ross' back. Then I kissed Ross. When I leaned back from the kiss, I waited for them to kiss each other. Brian was tentative, but Ross knew what he wanted.

Ross dipped his tongue into Brian's mouth while I slipped my hand down the back of Brian's pants. He moaned and I relaxed. I'd been afraid that Brian was just doing this because I wanted it. That he might not even enjoy it. But his moan made his feelings clear.

If I had any doubts about the threesome, they disappeared as the Quaalude kicked in. It seemed the most natural thing in the world. The kind of thing that should happen every time three guys had dinner. In fact, if more people had group sex the world would be a better place.

Maybe there'd be less war and stuff. Okay, I knew I was high when that thought popped into my head.

Brian's hands roamed Ross's body. Ross went to the Y six times a week. He was proud of his arms. Brian seemed to enjoy his large, well-defined biceps. I undid the front of Brian's pants. Reaching in, I grabbed his thick, uncut cock. He was half-hard and growing in my hand. Ross liked a little dirty talk. It wasn't really my thing, but I always tried to oblige him, so I leaned over and whispered into Ross' ear, "Feel his cock. It's already getting hard."

Ross' hand joined mine, pulling on Brian's dick. He said, "Oh, my God," and looked down. "I love foreskin." Ross dropped to his knees and began to nibble on Brian's extra skin. "I love your cock," he murmured between mouthfuls.

I looked at Brian, his blue eyes searching mine. Leaning over, I kissed him long and deep. He put his hands around my neck and pulled me close. I felt Ross opening my jeans and pulling my dick out. I looked down and watched as he sucked on me for a few moments, then switched back to Brian. Holding both cocks by the base, Ross enthusiastically sucked one, then the other.

I liked the show, but decided to recast the players. I lifted Ross to a standing position. Kissing him, I undid his jeans and pulled out his cock. It was long, thin, and freckled around the base. I started jerking it. Placing a hand on Brian's shoulder, I eased him down. I guided Ross' dick into his mouth. Brian closed his eyes and took Ross in deep. He moaned a bit as he did so.

I kissed Ross, then pulled his shirt over his head. With one hand, I guided Brian over to suck my cock. I reached down and jerked Ross while I closed my eyes and concentrated on the velvet sensation of Brian's mouth.

Brian moved back and forth between Ross and me, sucking my dick, then Ross'. Back and forth until I guided Brian back to a standing position, then pushed him down onto the mattress. I stepped out of my jeans. Brian pulled the rest of his clothes off. I crawled onto the mattress and lifted his cock until it was standing straight up in the air. I ran my tongue up and down the shaft, then Ross joined me and we were on either side of Brian's prick, our lips meeting occasionally in a glancing kiss.

Brian took Ross and me by the hair and pressed our faces together. We kissed, deeply, passionately. I liked thinking that Brian was watching, getting excited by our kiss. Then Brian rolled over and raised his ass in the air. I got up off the mattress and opened the top drawer of the dresser. I fished around until I found a jar of Vaseline.

Getting back on the bed, I greased up Brian's ass, dipping a finger into him just to hear him moan. I lubed up Ross' prick and led him over to Brian's ass. Ross pushed in slowly. "Oh yeah, it's tight. It's really tight."

Placing his hands on Brian's hips, Ross began pulling the boy back onto his prick, skewering him over and over again. I made my way to the other side of the mattress. Brian grabbed at my cock and pulled it into his mouth.

Every time Ross thrust into him, Brian took my cock deeper into his mouth. I slipped a hand behind Brian's head and held him down tight on my dick. I looked into Ross' dark eyes. He picked up his pace and pounded Brian faster and harder. Then his face crinkled in on itself, and I could tell he was coming deep inside Brian.

Brian pulled off my dick and looked over my shoulder as Ross gave him a few last pumps. Then Brian flipped himself over and offered his ass to me. "Fuck me," he demanded in the harshest voice I'd ever heard him use. "Come on, fuck me."

Seconds later I was inside of him.

"Yeah. Hard. Fuck me hard."

I pounded into him as viciously as I could, and he asked for more again and again. With one hand he jacked himself off. His strokes were fast and angry, his fist pounding down again and again. Ross tried to kiss him, but my fucking him kept him bouncing around on the bed.

Then I was coming. The spunk ripped out of me, leaving a trail of pleasure and pain as it splashed into Brian's ass. I kept pounding Brian a few more times until he exploded in wads of cum.

Ross and I flopped onto the bed next to Brian. None of us moved. As the sex faded, the Quaaludes kicked in, and we drifted off to sleep without even wiping ourselves off.

A few hours later, I woke up. Brian sat on the edge of the bed putting on his socks. I sat up next to him. "Sneaking off without a goodbye?"

"I didn't want to wake you."

"You had fun, didn't you?"

"It's not always about having fun. Sometimes it's about more than that."

I didn't know what to say. He wanted more from me. I didn't offer it.

"You don't really care one way or the other, do you?"

"Life is easier that way," I said honestly.

He called me an asshole and left. I didn't think he'd be coming back. I felt relieved and sad and happy that I'd only damaged him a tiny, tiny bit. I didn't especially like being called an asshole, but I figured it was the better way to be. I could have been nicer to Brian, told him some of the things he wanted to hear, lied to him to be polite. Let him down easy, as they say. But the one who'd feel better would be me.

If I'd set this up so Brian walked away thinking I was a great guy, then he'd spend his time trying to figure out how to get me back, or worse, wondering what was wrong with him that a great guy like me didn't fall in love with him. Not that I thought being an asshole did him any favors, it just hurt less in the long run.

Ross rolled over and slipped his hand between my legs, cupping my dick in his palm.

# # #

We woke up late the next morning and took a shower. One of the things I liked most about Ross was that he had a boyfriend, meaning he wasn't around much during the week. But this was Tuesday morning, and I was beginning to wonder why he was still here. While I was shampooing his hair, I asked, "How's Earl?"

"Jealous, hopefully."

"So, this isn't about me."

Ross kissed me and said, "Only marginally."

When we got out of the shower, he said, "I'm going with you. I want to hear what Bernie has to say. I want to catch whoever did this."

"Shouldn't you be looking for a job?"

"I can do that tomorrow."

I didn't want a partner. I wanted time by myself so I could think things through, but it seemed there wasn't a way to get rid of Ross. I liked him. In fact, I liked him a lot. I even liked having him around. But not when I was working.

As we drove out to the Kennedy heading to the south side, Ross told me what he thought of Brian. "He's a nice kid. Very sexy. But I don't think he's for you."

"I think he figured that out last night."

"Oh? Something happened?" When I didn't answer, he guessed. "He wasn't there when I woke up. I suppose that means something, doesn't it?"

"Congratulations, you're a detective," I said dryly.

The Kennedy turned into the Dan Ryan, and we took that all the way down to The University of Chicago. The campus was enormous, and we found the parking structure with some difficulty. Worse, there were several hospitals that made up the Medical Center. The buildings come from various architectural periods, and their placement follows no obvious logic. We weren't even sure what the name of the hospital was, so we were reduced to asking people where they kept the burn patients.

After almost a half an hour, we stumbled upon an information desk and found out we, coincidentally, were in the right spot. The volunteer looked up Bernie's name and sent us to the fifth floor. Hospitals are uncomfortable places, they're all linoleum and poorly chosen pastel colors; everything was designed to be easily cleaned, which only left me feeling that the whole place was covered with a thick, slimy film of soap.

Walking into Bernie's room, the first thing I noticed was the dour-looking kid sitting next to the bed. In his early twenties, he was good looking, or at least he would have been if he'd smiled. There was something a little hulking about him, and I had the feeling he'd slouch when he stood up. His hands were over-large, as were his feet. He seemed uncomfortable and awkward in his body, as though he'd had a growth spurt just last summer.

I turned and looked at Bernie. He was sitting up in bed. His head was bandaged, as was more than half his face, his neck, and his left arm down to his wrist. Some of the exposed skin showed angry and pink, as though he'd gotten a bad sunburn. The eye I could see was hazy with pain medication.

He tried to smile when he saw us. "Hey, thanks for coming by." He turned to the guy sitting next to his bed. "Edward, this is Nick and Ross."

"Bernie," I said, then waited for him to actually look at me. "Davey asked me to look into the fire. I'm gonna need to ask some questions."

"I don't know if he's ready yet," Edward said.

"Do you feel up to it, Bernie?"

"I don't remember much," Bernie said. "I'm sorry."

I turned to Edward and said, "I wonder if we could talk alone."

"No," said Bernie. "I need Edward."

I didn't like it, but what could I do? Throw the guy out the window?

"Why were you still in the bar?"

Edward answered for him. "We'd had a fight. He was spending the night in the storeroom." Bernie didn't look at me, but he nodded agreement as Edward spoke.

"You finished your shift, and the bar closed. What happened next?" I'd left the question as open as I could so that Edward would have difficulty answering for Bernie.

"I...um, I did my side work. Got a blanket outta the office..." He paused, struggling with the pain medication. "... my coat. I got my coat. Went to the storeroom. Put some boxes together. I rolled up my coat up for a pillow."

"Then what?" I asked.

He looked for a moment like he didn't understand the question. But he continued, "I slept. Later, I heard noise and everything was on fire."

"What was the fight about?"

"What fight? There was no—"

"It was my fault," Edward said. "It was stupid. You know, who cleans the kitchen, who does the laundry. That kind of fight." He sighed heavily. It was a terrible thing to think about, that a fight about chores had led to permanent disfigurement.

I looked back at Bernie. "So, you have no idea who started the fire."

He shook his head a little, but it caused him pain. "No," he said.

"A couple of the stools got knocked over before the fire started. Do you have any idea why?"

Bernie was quiet for a long time. He didn't look at any of us. "To be honest, I don't remember very much of what happened. I went to sleep, and everything between then and Sunday afternoon is kind of gone."

Pain and trauma were good time erasers, but twelve hours seemed like a lot. I wasn't sure whether to believe him. I was out of questions, but we stayed a while longer. Ross and Bernie were friends. It would have been awkward to leave when the questions ran out.

"Are the drugs good?" Ross asked.

"Demerol," Bernie said.

"Cool."

Ross offered to bring anything Bernie wanted the next time he came, but Bernie said, "Edward gets me everything. He takes good care of me."

Ross and I walked out of the room and headed toward the elevator. On our way, we walked by a waiting room. As we did, a kid about twenty-five stuck his head out and said, "Excuse me, are you Ross?"

Ross turned and nodded.

"I'm Larry. Is Edward still in there with him?"

Ross nodded.

"Shit. I haven't been able to see Bernie at all. How is he? Does he look okay?"

"You should probably go home," Ross told him. Larry turned and went back to his seat in the waiting room.

When we got to the elevator, I asked Ross, "So, who's Larry?"

"The reason Bernie was fighting with Edward."

"I should talk to Edward again. Where does he live?"

"Shit, I should know that," Ross said. "Bernie used to live up in Evanston, but then he moved in with Edward. I don't remember if he told me where."

"Find out for me."

# # #

Ross had to check in with his boyfriend, so I had the evening free. I decided I'd get a feeling for the Surfside Neighborhood Association by taking in their meeting. They met in the fellowship room of a large, Gothic-looking church on LaSalle near the south end of Lincoln Park. Nearly two dozen people, mostly white, though some black, sat on uncomfortable, metal folding chairs.

Waiting for things to start, I felt like Ava Gardner. Well, not Ava herself, but a character she played in a Sunday afternoon movie Daniel had made me watch. She played a singer on a riverboat who, though she was really black, passed for white. All hell broke loose when people found out the truth. People noticed that I was new. But I passed, so they gave me pleasant smiles, assuming that I was an upset heterosexual just like them, there to run fags out of the neighborhood. I worried that one of the older women might chat me up, eventually pulling out a photo of some unfortunate single daughter or niece in need of a husband. The meeting began, so I was spared.

John Bradford was a red-faced man about my own age with a scraggly beard, aviator glasses, and a potbelly. He was dressed in a three-piece suit. The look didn't fit.

He seemed like a teenager playing at being adult. He stood behind a table and began the meeting briskly. A secretary sat next to him taking notes. The meeting had an obvious structure. He began by discussing the business of the previous meeting in which it had apparently been decided they would begin a letter-writing campaign to their local alderman. He stopped partway through and said, "As I'm sure most of you know, we've been given a tremendous opportunity to rid our neighborhood of this unpleasant annoyance."

The group erupted into sudden applause. Weakly, I applauded with them. I wondered if I was applauding a twist of fate or the actual arsonist sitting somewhere in the room.

"Therefore," Bradford continued, "we should reconsider the thrust of our letter-writing campaign, as well as other actions we planned to take in the next six months. Politicians hate to shut down successful businesses, especially when that business makes the right contributions. But it's a much simpler thing to keep a business from opening at all."

When he finished his statement, he opened the floor for discussion of steps that could be taken to prevent the reopening of Paradise Isle. What I found most disturbing about the discussion was its civility. No one used the terms faggot or queer or even pervert. Instead, they talked about negative influence on the neighborhood, sound pollution, damage to property values; the closest they came to being offensive was when one older woman stood up and began to talk about morality.

Her insistence that they deserved to win because they had the moral high ground was shot out of the water a few minutes later when a young, preppy type stood up and suggested, "In order to rebuild, they're going to need permits and building inspections and fire inspections and who knows what else. Isn't there a way we can influence whether the permits are given or the inspections passed?"

Immediately, Bradford whispered something to the secretary and she stopped taking notes. He stood quietly a moment, measuring his words. "That's always a possibility, though I'm not sure we have the necessary funds for that kind of...influence."

Quickly, they realized they didn't have the funds to "influence persuasively" and began to discuss fundraising opportunities. Bake sales and car washes were suggested. The idea of baking cookies so you could out-bribe a business you didn't care for made me miss the open, in-your-face hatred of people like my Uncle Jack. Somehow it seemed more honest.

I got up and waited outside. In the cold, I leaned against my car across the street from the church. About four cigarettes later, the meeting broke up and people began to trickle out of the old church. It was odd that I hadn't interviewed any of them the morning after the fire. Presumably some of them lived in The Shore. I wondered for a moment if they'd had a meeting in which they'd discussed ways to "remove" Paradise Isle from their neighborhood, and then, after the successful removal, had all met for breakfast to celebrate.

Finally, John Bradford came out. The secretary was with him, and the two were speaking softly to each other. I crossed the street and called out his name. He stared at me blankly.

"I'm Nick Nowak, I'm a private investigator looking into the Paradise Isle fire."

"And you snuck into our meeting."

"Your flier said it was open to all."

"You live in the neighborhood?"

"No, but—"

"Then it wasn't open to you. Please don't come back." He turned on his heel and began to walk away.

I followed. "I'd like to ask you some questions about your group." He hooked his arm in the secretary's elbow and picked up his speed, practically dragging the woman along with him. "Do you think anyone in your group is capable of arson?"

Ignoring me, he continued to run-walk down the icy street. I hoped the two might slip and give me an opportunity to question them.

"Mr. Bradford, is anyone in your group unstable or prone to violence?"

They turned a corner and stopped in front of a beat-up maroon Chevy Malibu. Bradford fumbled with his keys.

"Come on," I implored. "Someone got hurt, hurt pretty bad. Do you really think that's okay?"

He turned on me, his face so red it seemed to pulse. "If you ever come to another of our meetings, I'm going to call the cops." Then, shockingly, he spit on me. It hit me on the chest. I suppose it could have been a lot worse, but still I took a disgusted step back. Bradford got into his car and leaned over to unlock the passenger side. They closed up the doors, and he started the engine.

As he was about to pull away, I stepped forward and kicked a dent into his door. He turned and stared at me for a moment, then pulled out of the spot and drove away.

# # #

On Wednesday I had lunch with Davey to catch him up on what I'd learned. Unfortunately, I hadn't learned much. I knew the Outfit wasn't behind the fire, because his payments were up to date. They could have been lying, I suppose, but they wouldn't be collecting any money from Davey until the bar reopened, so there wasn't much motive there.

Something was funky with Bernie and his boyfriend, but I didn't know what. It might have just been that they didn't want to talk about their personal life. Given the complicated relationship they had going, it wasn't hard to figure out why they chose to lie. I had to admit, I'd be uncomfortable discussing my relationships—even without their being part of a criminal investigation.

John Bradford was now highest on my list of suspects. I told Davey about Bradford's performance the night before. I also mentioned the group's plan to out-bribe him when it came time to rebuild. He nodded, unsurprised. I doubted it was the first time he'd met that kind of resistance.

I wished I had more to implicate Bradford beyond his dislike of the bar and his bizarre behavior when I tried to talk to him. Neither were things I could take to the arson squad and get a decent hearing.

"He's never threatened you directly, has he? Sent you letters? Anything?"

"Once in awhile we get letters from freaks, but they don't sign them. Maybe they're from him. I don't know."

"Do you still have the letters?"

"Huh? Oh, no," he scoffed. "Why would I want to keep them?"

Davey was a wreck. All through lunch he'd been distracted and had difficulty following the things I was saying. I began to wonder if he'd taken something, or rather a little too much something, but then I thought, *No, the club is his life and it's gone for now. Someone took it away.* The poor guy was lost.

"I'll figure out what happened," I promised.

"I know. I didn't say you wouldn't," he said. He studied the table for a while, as though it had the answers to some secret test he was taking. "I don't know if I can do it. I don't know if I can reopen. It's like opening a whole new bar. I don't know if I can do it."

"Take a few days, Davey. Don't think about anything. Don't make decisions. Just forget everything."

"How do I do that?" he wondered.

I didn't have a good answer for him.

After lunch, I went home. I knew there had to be something productive I could do that afternoon that would help find the arsonist. I needed a list of everyone in the Surfside Neighborhood Association. I could focus on John Bradford, but it was just as likely that someone in his group might have done it and he was covering for them. Rationally, though, I couldn't investigate every person in the group. So would a list be that valuable? What I really needed was something to make the police look closely at the group. And I had no clue what that might be. I gave up and took a nap.

The phone woke me up just after the sun went down. Before I left the scene of the fire, I'd handed out a half dozen of my business cards to the firemen who were there. My business number was printed on the front and my home number handwritten on the back. Usually, handing out cards is a pointless exercise, but when I picked up the phone it was one of the firemen. He sounded nervous. "Do you have a car?" he asked.

"Yeah."

"Pick me up on the corner of Wrightwood and Orchard." Before I could even say yes, he'd hung up. There wasn't anything else to do except rush out of my apartment and find my car. About twenty minutes later I cruised down Wrightwood, slowing when I got near Orchard.

I was looking in the other direction when someone opened my passenger door and jumped in. I'd never even completely stopped. I studied the guy sitting in the passenger seat. He was the blue-eyed fireman I'd talked to the day of the fire. He wore a pair of dark blue pants that were part of his uniform and a matching T-shirt that was little too tight. He slouched down in the seat, trying not to be seen.

"What's your name?" I asked.

"Hank Withers."

"Thanks for calling me, Hank."

"Drive out of the neighborhood. I don't want anyone from the station seeing me." I was pretty sure the station was on Halsted a few blocks in the opposite direction. I kept going on Wrightwood, then took a left and headed north to Diversey.

"Why the cloak and dagger?"

"The arson guys have been putting pressure on us about your friend's case. They keep asking if the smoke was black. Some of the guys are starting to remember that it was."

"Is that important?" I asked.

"Black smoke means the fire was started with gasoline. I heard they have your guy charging a lot of gas on his gas card just the day before."

"He drives a Cadillac. He charges gas every other day."

"That's just what I heard."

"So, the smoke wasn't black?"

"No, it wasn't."

I swung a left on Diversey and headed the car toward the El stop near Sheffield.

"Where are you going?" Hank asked.

"I need a payphone. I've got to call Davey."

El stations pretty reliably have a working payphone. I found a parking spot on Wilton and jumped out. I ran around the corner to the station, dropped in my dime and made the call. Davey's answering machine picked up.

"Davey, are you there?" I asked. When he didn't pick up, I told the machine, "You need to get out of town. They're probably going to try for an arrest soon. It'll just be better if you're not here." I hung up.

Wilton was dark and quiet. I got back into the car and sat very still for a few moments. It gave me a chance to take a better look at Hank. Even though it was dark, I could see he was the kind of guy people call rugged. His hair was dishwater blond and close cropped, his face was covered in stubble most of the way up his cheeks, he had a dimple in his chin that was almost an exclamation point. His blue eyes caught mine, and I realized he'd been checking me out, too.

Sliding over the bench seat, he reached out and put his huge hand in my crotch. He rubbed my dick through the coarse denim until it was good and hard. Then he unzipped my Levis. He reached into my pants, through the opening in my boxers, and pulled out my cock.

"Nice," he mumbled. He started sucking me off. He had more enthusiasm than skill, but sometimes enthusiasm is plenty. Taking my cock all the way down his throat, he gagged. Instead of making him more hesitant, he chuckled deep in his throat and tried again. This time he got me much further down. Even in the dark, I could see that his face was red with effort.

I ran my hand across his wide shoulders. His throat was hot, and my cock felt like it was about to burn. He bobbed up and down faster and faster, my breathing increasing with his pace. My cock slipped out of his mouth; quickly he popped it back in.

"Slow down," I told him. "You're going to make me come too fast."

But he just made a noise halfway between a growl and a laugh. I was close. My prick rock hard, my hips lifting off the seat, toes curling in my boots. Hank sat back and pumped me with his big fist. Then I was coming, coming so hard and fast I hit myself in the chin.

Smiling, Hank kissed me, and with a couple swipes of his tongue licked the cum off my chin. "I have to go," he said. And with that he was out of my car and gone. I sat there in the sudden silence. If my cock weren't still sticky with semen and saliva, I'd wonder if it had actually happened.

# # #

Thursday, I spent the day in my office working on things I might actually get paid for. I was distracted, of course. My mind kept coming back to the fire. I hadn't heard from Davey, and I had no idea whether he'd left town or not. Obviously, there was a rush to figure out what happened, and part of me felt guilty for trying to keep a roof over my head. On the other hand, sometimes when you ignore a problem, that's when the solutions start to shake loose.

Unfortunately, it was nearly the end of the day and nothing had shaken loose. The phone rang, and I picked it up, "Nick Nowak."

"Hey," said Ross. "I've got Edward's address. Sorry it took so long. I finally had to call Miss Minerva."

I got a piece of paper and a pen. "Great. What is it?"

"You're not going to believe this, but Edward Wyznicki lives at The Shore, apartment 1113."

"You're kidding."

"Minerva said that's how Edward and Bernie met. Bernie started out on the happy hour shift. Edward kept stopping by after work. Two months later, Bernie moved in with him."

"What's this Edward guy do?"

"Works at First Chicago. Some kind of account manager."

"Thanks." I wasn't sure how important it was. My gut said the arsonist was someone in Bradford's group.

"Are you going to go see him?" There was too much eagerness in his voice.

"At some point."

"What are you going to do, then?"

I wasn't sure. "Go find Bradford, I guess. Try to talk to him again."

"I'll go with you."

"You're looking for a job, remember."

"I did that earlier."

"And tonight you're spending time with your boyfriend."

"Maybe later. He's on his way to a fundraiser for The Lincoln Park Zoo. 'Socialite Sugar Pilson donates millions to save the Siberian Meerkat.'" It sounded like he was kidding. But I didn't know enough about Sugar Pilson or Siberian Meerkats to be sure. Of course, I read "The Silver Spoon" and it sounded like the kind of thing Earl wrote about.

Detective work is ninety-nine percent boring and one percent the kind of excitement no one should ever experience. If this was going to fall into the one percent category, it would be happening soon, and I didn't want Ross in danger.

"Look, I think I should do the rest of this on my own," I said.

An unpleasant silence fell between us.

"Why?"

"I work better that way."

"You're always pushing people away."

I actually sat back in my chair when he said that. It was overkill, and far too personal for a conversation like this. Reluctantly, I let it pass.

"Why does this matter to you, Ross? You never showed much interest in my work before."

He was quiet. Then said, "I was supposed to close that night. Bernie was supposed to get off at two. But then Earl came in, and I begged Bernie to switch with me. He shouldn't have been there at all. It should have been me."

"But he didn't have anywhere to sleep," I pointed out. "He would have been there no matter what time he finished."

"That's not true. Larry was at the bar around one. He wanted to take Bernie home with him. But he lives out in Hinsdale and had to have breakfast in the morning with his parents, so he didn't want to wait."

I got that Ross felt guilty, that he wanted to do something. But it didn't change anything. I said, "Goodbye," and hung up.

I took the El up to Fullerton and switched trains so I could get to Diversey. When I got there, I walked the five blocks to the intersection of Diversey and Broadway. It began to drizzle again. I pulled my fleece collar up tight around my chin.

I figured the best way to deal with the Surfside Neighborhood Association was to show up at John Bradford's door and see if I could rattle him. Sure, he'd probably try to slam his door, but there are ways around that. Fortunately, I was wearing a pretty heavy pair of work boots.

When I got to The Shore, I buzzed Edward and Bernie's apartment. Even though my gut feeling was Edward didn't have much to tell me, I didn't like loose ends. Investigating a crime was about determining facts. Some facts eliminated possibilities. Others made them more likely. Following a gut feeling wasn't a bad idea if you followed it toward something. Following a gut feeling away from something was always a mistake. Besides, I wasn't looking forward to dealing with Bradford, and talking to Edward put it off for another twenty minutes.

Edward answered and asked who it was. I told him. After a long pause, the security door finally buzzed. I made my way to the rickety elevator and hit the call button. It clanked and groaned on its way down. The door opened. As the elevator climbed to the eleventh floor, every muscle in my body tensed, and I was sure that just a few feet above me, beyond the laminated ceiling of the car, there was a wire cable quickly unraveling and likely to break.

Fortunately, at the eleventh floor, I pulled the metal grate to one side, pushed the door open, and stepped out. Safe.

Breathing a sigh of relief, I set about finding 1113. It was toward the front of the building, on the side I hadn't canvassed. I knocked on the door. Edward appeared in just a few seconds. He invited me in and offered me a seat.

The apartment was a one bedroom with a view of the courtyard and not much else. Edward and Bernie had decorated in a few quick trips to The Great Ace. Seemingly, they'd bought all the furniture recommended for apartment dwellers and nothing took up more space than it needed to. Along one living room wall sat a sofa-bed made from a collapsible metal frame and a canvas-covered futon that appeared to be bent onto the frame against its will. There were a couple metal stools, a glass coffee table, a set of gray metal shelves where the TV and stereo were located, and a tiny but functional dinette set with two chairs. There were framed pictures of Edward and Bernie scattered about. One of them had a nasty crack in the glass, possibly from being thrown across the room.

"What's this about?" Edward asked. "Bernie's okay, isn't he?"

"I'm sure Bernie's fine," I said. "I just have a few questions to clear up."

"I really don't know anything. I mean, he's been too doped up to say much."

"Where were you when the fire started?" I asked.

Tears began to fall down his face. "Here," he managed to choke out.

"Do you own a down jacket?"

He shrugged. "Yeah, they're warm." They were warm. That's why half the people in Chicago had them. I wasn't sure his having one meant anything.

"Do you want to tell me again why the two of you were fighting?" I asked.

"Household chores. I told you."

"It didn't bother you that Bernie was fucking around on you with another guy?"

Edward sniffled a few times and went pale. "Of course it bothered me. I love him."

"That's what the fight was about, wasn't it?"

"What difference does it make?" He seemed a little annoyed that I kept asking.

"Obviously it makes a difference. You lied about it."

"Privacy. Don't we deserve privacy?"

"I wish I could leave you alone, but the police are trying to blame someone who didn't do this. Someone who's innocent."

Edward took a big gulp of air and tried to stop crying. "It's my fault. Don't you see that?"

For a moment, I thought he might be confessing. "Why is it your fault?" I asked.

"It's my fault Bernie was there when the fire started."

I nodded. "You threw him out, and he had nowhere else to go." Not entirely true. He could have gone to his boyfriend's if he'd left the bar earlier.

"It's my fault." Then he broke down completely. He was a sobbing, soggy mess. I didn't know what else to do but put my hand on the guy's shoulder. That just made him cry harder.

I felt bad. Not only was I wasting my time, I was torturing the poor guy. I said my goodbyes and got out of the apartment.

Bradford lived in 304, two floors below Ruthie. I managed to survive the elevator ride down and walked over to his door. I braced myself for the anger I expected when he saw me and knocked. A few moments later the door flew open. Bradford looked up and focused on me. "Oh no, no way. Screw you."

He tried to slam the door, but I'd managed to get my foot in between the door and the jam. Unfortunately, most of my leg was in there, too, and the door slammed on my knee. Ignoring the pain, I forced the door open again.

I realized Bradford was wearing a big, puffy down coat; obviously on his way out somewhere. "Nice coat," I said.

"I'm calling the cops," Bradford shrilled, then began to head for the heavy black phone sitting on a small table.

"Thanks, I'd like to talk to them. I've got a witness who saw someone coming out of Paradise right after the fire stared wearing a coat just like the one you've got on."

Bradford paled. "A lot of people have coats like this."

"Yeah, but it'll be enough to get the cops to look closely at you and your group," I pointed out.

"I don't get it. Why are you doing this? You seem like a decent enough guy. They can't be paying you that much—"

"A decent enough guy, what does that mean?" I knew exactly what it meant.

"I mean you're not..." His voice trailed off as he realized what was going on. "Oh, I see," he said finally.

"You want to call the police now, or do you want me to do it?"

Behind me, the elevator began to rise to another floor. It was loud. It sounded like a train going by. I'd been too focused on surviving the ride to realize. I looked at the wall behind me for a moment, then asked Bradford, "Is it always that loud?"

He shrugged. "They can't manage to get it fixed. They promise—"

Without a word, I walked away from him. Quickly, I hurried to the stairwell. Bradford called after me, "Don't come back again or I will call the police! You got that?"

I ran up the stairs two at time. On the fifth floor, I hurried to Ruthie's door. I knocked nervously. This would clinch it. If Ruthie answered the way I thought she would, I had Bradford. The police would be arresting him within the hour.

The old woman opened the door and looked up at me. "Ruthie, the guy you saw...you knew he lived here because you heard the elevator. You saw him come toward the building and then you heard the elevator."

"Yes," she said, giving me a look that suggested that I should have known that all along.

"He lives below you, right?"

She stunned me by shaking her head and pointed a finger to the ceiling.

I hurried back to the elevator. Pressing the button over and over, I nearly knocked a woman over when the door finally opened. The ride was unbearable. We stopped on the seventh floor, and the woman got out. I shut the grate behind her and pounded on the button marked eleven.

It was Edward. That's all I kept thinking. I'd been so sure it was Bradford. I'd wanted it to be Bradford, so I didn't see the truth in front of me. Edward had started the fire in a fit of jealousy. He'd been saying it was his fault, and he meant that it was his fault. He did it.

Finally, I got to the eleventh floor. Bolted out of the elevator. Pounded on the door to 1113. "Edward! Edward, open the door." There wasn't any response. I knocked a few more times, then tried the doorknob to see if it might open. It did. I stepped into Edward's living room. Everything looked the same, except for a piece of paper, a letter, on the coffee table. I walked over and read it. It was short.

It read, "I'm sorry. To everyone who ever loved me. I'm sorry. It has to be this way."

Suddenly, the many ways to kill yourself in your own home started popping into my head. Gas in the kitchen. But I'd smell it. Knives, also in the kitchen. I peeked in. No bloody corpse laid out on the floor. Pills. People got in bed after they took them. I hurried into the bedroom. The bed was empty. Nicely made. That left the bathroom. Slit wrists in the bathtub. I pushed the door open, sure that I was going to see a tub full of bloody water. But it was empty. The bathroom was empty.

Edward wasn't in the apartment. Anywhere. But he'd left the note. A thought flashed through my head. The roof! I ran out of the apartment. I didn't have the patience to wait for the ancient elevator. I bolted to the stairs and dashed up the four floors to the roof.

When I got to the top, the door to the roof was open. I rushed out. There was a two-foot yellow brick continuation of the outer wall running all the way around the roof. Fine gravel covered the surface. There were a few bits of un-melted snow in the corners. Tar had been applied liberally in various spots.

Edward stood on the west side of the building. From where he stood, he could stare down at Paradise. I quietly walked closer to him. When I was about ten feet away, I stopped and said, "Edward. Why don't you come away from there?"

He turned to face me, tears streaming down his face. "It wasn't supposed to happen this way. Bernie called me around one that morning. He wanted to come home. I told him he couldn't. He couldn't ever come home. He said he'd be there. That he was staying there. If I changed my mind I could call him. That's when I decided. I wanted us to die together. I love him, but...he'd ruined everything. I wanted to die with him. But I got scared. I'm a coward. I ran out of there. I left him."

"He didn't die, though. He's okay. So it's over."

"No! He's not okay...his face...I ran away."

Daniel flashed into my mind. His face bashed by a metal baseball bat. His hand covering what was likely permanent damage. I've never even tried—

"Hurting yourself won't make anything better," I practically yelled at Edward. "Come away from the edge."

I took another step closer to him.

"STOP! STOP IT! You don't know. You don't know what it's like." In a burst, he began to sob. "You don't know."

I went with the only thing I could think of. "Edward, Bernie loves you. He's been lying to protect you. Doesn't that mean he loves you?"

"He let me into the bar. He trusted me! Then he went into the storeroom and I poured booze all over and...I lit it. I lit it on fire."

"Edward, this is as bad as it gets. It gets better from here. It does." I promised, but wasn't sure it was true.

"I can't...I just can't..."

"Yes, you can..."

He didn't jump. He sat. It looked as though he was trying to sit on the short wall behind him and simply missed. Bending his knees, he let himself fall backward until the backs of his calves hit the wall and his feet flipped up into the air.

Edward was gone.

# # #

A few days later, my fireman called and wanted to come by. Things had calmed down. Bernie admitted what really happened, so the police stopped trying to pin the whole thing on Davey. Davey offered to pay me my salary until Paradise Isle reopened as a thank you. I took him up on half pay. His insurance covered Miss Minerva's record collection, and she planned to spend a delirious week replacing music she liked and buying new music she was sure to. Ross got a waiter job at The French Bakery on

Brian's recommendation, which was a little weird for me, but hey, whatever.

I treated myself to the cassette of a Keith Jarrett concert recorded in Germany. I'd been listening to it on my boom box over and over again. It probably would have sounded a whole lot better on vinyl, but that would require replacing the stereo that had been ripped off the January before. The music was melancholy without being depressing. It was playing when Hank got there.

Brian thought I was still in love with my ex. He'd said so in a letter he taped to my door; a goodbye letter that explained, from his perspective, why things hadn't worked out between us. Maybe he's right. Or maybe I've just lost the taste for love. Love isn't always a good thing. Sometimes it makes a mess of people's lives. Like it did for Bernie and Edward. Still, I was excited that Hank was there. He'd been a stand-up guy, letting me know what the cops were trying to do to Davey. So I was thinking, who knows, maybe love isn't so bad. Actually, it might even be fun.

When I answered the door, Hank stood there all decked out like he was on his way to fighting a fire, except for the gym bag he held in one hand. He tipped his helmet at me and said, "You want to show me where the hot spots are?"

I chuckled and led him into my apartment. We didn't get past the living room before he dropped his gym bag and was on me. I kissed him and tried to feel him through the thick, canvas-like material of his jacket, but it was too heavy. The whole outfit was yellow, with reinforced patches and large pockets. He wore a pair of heavy, black, rubberized boots. I reached up to take his helmet off, and he stopped me, "Oh, no, you don't."

He pushed me into one of my director's chairs and then stepped back so I could get a good view of him. First, he slowly pulled off the heavy gloves that protected his hands. Then, one by one, he unclasped the hooks on his jacket. As it fell open, I got a glimpse of skin. Not surprisingly, he was naked under his outer gear. I wondered if that was regulation.

He dropped the jacket to the floor. Suspenders held up his pants. Obviously, they had weights at the firehouse, and Hank spent time using them. His chest was big, with pectoral muscles like slabs of meat. His upper arms were huge. Even his forearms were big. He lifted a foot and put his boot in my lap. "Pull." I pulled. The boot popped off in my hand. He put his other foot in my lap. I have to say that his striptease was a little odd, since it was being accompanied by improvisational jazz piano. But that didn't seem to dampen his enjoyment. Or, for that matter, mine.

Hank dropped one suspender over his impressive shoulder. Then the other. He unbuckled his pants. I waited for them to fall, but they only slid down a few inches. The material was so thick the pants could stand on their own. Finally, he pushed them down to the floor.

His large thighs squeezed together naturally, and his cock popped out in front of them. He stepped out of his pants and knelt in front of me. Quickly, he undid my jeans and pulled them down to my knees. He popped my dick into his mouth and sucked me with the same enthusiasm he'd shown in the car. I rested a hand on his helmet as he bobbed up and down.

I leaned back and closed my eyes. I concentrated on the feeling of my dick sliding in and out of his mouth. Suddenly, it stopped. Hank stood up and took a few steps backward. He got on the floor on top of his gear. "Come here."

I stood up and wiggled out of my pants. I pulled my T-shirt over my head. Naked, I joined him on the floor. He kissed me deeply, shoving his tongue in and out of my mouth. "I want you to fuck me."

I didn't need to be asked twice. I started to get up and go for the Vaseline, but he stopped me by pulling me back down. "It's okay. I'm ready."

I wasn't sure what he meant at first, but when I lifted his legs into the air and went to stick my cock in, I found that he'd already lubed himself up.

"I like a man who comes prepared," I said.

He smiled and inhaled sharply as I pushed all the way into him. His cock was nice and rigid as it flopped around on his belly. Hooking his feet around my neck, he lifted his ass up to meet me. "Oh, God, yes."

I pounded into him again and again. Sweat broke out on my forehead. I wrapped my hands around his thick thighs and pulled him to me. Hank approached getting fucked with the same enthusiasm he had giving out a blow job. However, while he'd seemed a bit inexperienced with oral sex, he was either very experienced with fucking or a complete natural. Each time I thrust into him, his hips came up to meet me.

Bucking and twisting beneath me, his helmet soon came off and rolled around on the floor near his head. I reached around his leg and started jacking him off. His prick was rocket-shaped, with a thick stalk tapering down to a smaller head.

I was close, but I wanted him to come first. Closing my eyes, I tried counting backward from a hundred. Ninety-nine. Ninety-eight. Ninety-seven. Suddenly, his ass clamped down on my cock, and he was coming all over my fist. I let go and came deep inside of him.

Collapsing on him, I lay there sweaty and sticky with his cum. "That was incredible," I murmured. I kind of liked this guy and was beginning to hope he'd be coming around a lot.

"Do you mind if I take a shower?" he asked. "I can't go home covered in spunk."

And then I realized how little I knew about Hank.

"Who's at home?"

"Wife and kids."

"Ah," I said. "Yeah, go ahead. Take a shower."

"You wanna join me?"

"I'm fine, thanks."

Little Boy Fallen

Always be careful who you trick with. I should have that tattooed on my forehead so I can see it every morning when I shave.

The woman was waiting for me when I got to my office. She looked to be in her late forties, thick around the hips, busty. There was lot of red lipstick caked onto her lips, and her hair was done up in a way that had probably gotten a lot of attention during the Eisenhower administration. At first, I thought she was a patient of the dentist down the hall, but when I pulled my keys out and started to unlock the door, she came over.

"Are you Mr. Nowak?" she asked.

A few weeks shy of my thirty-third birthday, I didn't much like being called 'mister' by anyone who wasn't still in grammar school. "You can call me Nick."

I opened the door and led her into my tiny office. The furniture was crammed together, and still I had room left over for a dead corn plant in one corner. The window was big, taking up most of the outer wall. Eight floors below was LaSalle Street. Across the way stood an ultra-modern, steel and glass building that was so tall it cut out most of my light.

"He said you were nice," she commented, while making herself comfortable in my guest chair. She wore a red cloth coat with a white fox collar. Instead of a purse, she carried a photo album, clutching it tight to her chest.

I hung my suede jacket on the back of my door and pulled a box of Marlboros out of the pocket. I decided not to ask who 'he' was. Not yet. Instead, I asked, "What's your name, ma'am?"

"Helen Borlock." I sat down at my desk and lit a cigarette while she talked. "He told me to come. He said you'd help. You can help, can't you?"

"I don't know if I can help," I said honestly. "I don't know why you're here."

She gave me a confused look, as though I should know why she was there. "Bobby told me to come. He said you'd help."

"Bobby who?"

"Bobby Martin."

I was pretty sure I didn't know a Bobby Martin and said so.

"Bobby was my son's roommate. One of them, I mean. There were four of them living there. Sweet boys, always laughing. The apartment is on Clark and Fullerton. They did it up nice. Every room a different color."

I still hadn't a clue who she was talking about.

Abruptly, she held out the photo album. "This is my Lenny." To be polite, I took the album. "I never wanted to name him Leonard. My husband insisted. He'd had a friend, in the Marines. Wanted to name his son Leonard, after his friend. The friend died, you see."

I flipped the album open. There was Helen with an infant. I was right. In her day, Helen had been a looker. I flipped a few pages and Lenny began to grow up. Looked like he was on his way to being a looker, too.

"What is it Bobby thought I could help you with?"

She glanced out the window like she suddenly needed to check the weather. It was overcast and threatening to rain or, worse, throw in one last snowstorm for the winter. After a little sigh, she said, "Three weeks ago, my son was murdered."

"Mrs. Borlock, I'm a private investigator. I don't investigate murders. The police do that."

"They don't care. Lenny is just another pervert to them."

I waited a few moments, considering. I was telling her the truth. It wasn't the kind of thing I did. Or at least tried not to do. Mainly I did background checks, skip traces, once in a while a little surveillance. That was it. Murder was different. Yes, I used to be a policeman, but I'd only worked a beat. I'd never been a detective. In the nearly six years I spent on the job, when it came to murder I'd never done much more than secure a crime scene and make sure witnesses stayed put.

"Can you afford a private investigator?"

"Yes. I always put a little aside for Lenny. Ever since he was a little boy." She stared at her hands, which seemed particularly empty now that I was flipping through the photo album. "I used to think I'd give him the money on his wedding. He was sixteen when I figured out that was never going to happen, so for a while I thought I'd give him the money to go to college. But he was never book smart. Last couple of years, I've been waiting to see, did he maybe want to start a business or get a nice beau and buy a house." Her voice turned bitter. "I should have given it to him. Should have let him spend on whatever he wanted."

She looked like she might break down, but fortunately she didn't. I took the final drag off my cigarette and stubbed it out. Against my better judgment, I said, "Tell me what happened to Lenny."

"Someone pushed him off the seventh floor of the atrium at Water Tower."

That seemed pretty cut and dried. "Were there witnesses?"

"It was a little after ten in the morning."

"No one saw him being pushed?"

She shook her head.

"So, how do you know he was pushed?"

Mrs. Borlock pursed her lips. Tears popped into her eyes and threatened to spill over onto her cheeks. "You're going to tell me my boy killed himself, just like the police."

"Right now, I'm not telling you anything. Right now, I'm asking questions. How do you know he was pushed?"

"I just know," she spat. "I know Lenny. And he wouldn't kill himself."

"Why wouldn't Lenny kill himself?" I was expecting a lame answer, like she'd raised him as a good Catholic, and, since it was against God's law, he wouldn't do it. But she didn't say that. She said something completely different.

"Lenny was the happiest person I ever met."

# # #

That afternoon, I hopped on the El and got off at Diversey rather than going all the way to my regular stop at Belmont. I turned away from DePaul and walked toward the lake. Mrs. Borlock had given me the address of the apartment her son shared with three roommates, one of whom was the mysterious Bobby Martin.

At first, I wasn't sure it had been a good idea to take the case. Logic told me the kid had killed himself. Yes, his mother thought he was the happiest person she'd ever met. But suicidal tendencies are exactly the kind of thing children hide from their parents. If the police thought it was suicide, then in all likelihood it was suicide. I had my issues with the Chicago PD, but that didn't mean they did sloppy work.

So, why'd I take the case? Mrs. Helen Borlock, that's why. Someone needed to help her. Not to find her son's murderer; there was no murderer. She didn't understand why her son killed himself, and she needed to understand. She needed the reason. As I rang the bell to her son's apartment, I promised myself I'd find it for her.

I got buzzed into the building and climbed the stairs. On the second floor, a door sprang open and a boy in his early twenties stood there looking me up and down. He had short brown hair, a heavy five o'clock shadow, a small moustache hanging out beneath his nose on what looked like a temporary basis, and a pair of impossibly large glasses. He was short, real short. About five four, which made me nearly a foot taller. He was wearing a pair of gray gym shorts with the name of some high school partially rubbed off and not much else. He had decent legs and a tight chest, both covered with lots of dark hair. In the background, the Go-Gos got the beat.

"You're not Bobby, are you?" I asked, though I was pretty sure I'd have remembered him if he was.

"I'm Freddie. Who are you?" Without waiting to find out, he turned and went back into the apartment. I followed him in. The living room was painted an antacid pink. Over an aqua-colored vinyl sofa that looked like it was stolen from a bus station was a large painting. Globs of paint arranged themselves to form a large, erect, rainbow penis. At its base, the painter had glued several handfuls of what looked like dryer lint.

Freddie lifted the needle off the record and the Go-Gos were silenced. He gave me the once-over a second time. "You're looking for Bobby? Why? Did someone send you as a present? He'll be—"

"I'm Nick Nowak. I'm a private investigator. Mrs. Borlock hired me to look into Lenny's death."

"Oh, my." Behind his glasses he blinked a few times. He was one of those guys with eyelashes so dark and thick it made you wonder if he was wearing mascara.

"What's your last name, Freddie?"

"Twombly," he said. "Isn't it terrible? It sounds like I'm lisping. Even when I'm not." He lit an extra-long cigarette. I decided to be sociable and pulled out my Marlboros.

"You mind if I ask you a few questions?"

"Only if they're personal," he said playfully. He hooked a finger into the elastic band of his shorts, dragging them down over his hip. I struggled to keep my focus on lighting my cigarette.

"Why do you think Lenny killed himself?" It was the question of the hour, so I figured I'd start there.

Freddie stopped being playful and sat on the sofa. It squeaked. "I don't think Lenny killed himself. No one thinks that."

I had hoped it would be easier than this. "Why do you say that?"

"Jumping? At Water Tower? It's so dramatic. Lenny wasn't a drama queen. Actually, I'm the drama queen in the house. Everything upsets me, but nothing upset Lenny. He was always mellow."

"So, what do you think happened?"

Freddie shrugged. "Isn't it your job to figure that out?"

"Do you mind if I look at Lenny's room? And then maybe ask you a few more questions?"

He picked up the ashtray and walked out of the room. "Come on. It's this way. Lenny and I share a room."

I followed Freddie down the hallway. Just above the waistband of his shorts, he had dimples in the small of his back, one on each side. Halfway down the hall he turned, and we were in a small bedroom crammed with two twin mattresses, a schoolhouse desk, and another penis picture with lint for pubic hair—this one was flaccid.

The walls were painted an electric blue, and the ceiling was black. One of the mattresses was stripped naked, showing its sweat stains. The other wore pink polka-dotted sheets. On the bare mattress was a box filled with odds and ends from around the apartment—a frying pan, a picture, some juice glasses from the fifties.

Freddie watched as I looked over the room. I didn't know exactly what I was looking for. Hints, I suppose, little clues as to why Lenny might have killed himself: angry letters from creditors, love letters from a failed romance, the complete works of Sylvia Plath. Anything.

"Did Lenny have money problems?" I asked.

"It's a two-bedroom apartment and there are four of us. We all have money problems." I looked into the closet. "The left side is his," Freddie volunteered.

"What about boyfriends? Was he involved with anyone?"

"No. Lenny had sex. He tricked and stuff, but there wasn't anyone serious."

I moved Lenny's clothes around. Stuck my hand in the pockets of his coats. Freddie continued chattering. "I used to be Bobby's boyfriend. So did Chuck, our other roommate, but only for about five minutes. Bobby tricked with Lenny, which is what broke Bobby and I up, though at this point I can't remember why I cared." He gasped suddenly. "Oh, my God! You're gonna think I killed Lenny for having sex with Bobby! That's just ridiculous. It was a year and a half ago for God's sake. In gay years that's like a decade. Besides I have an alibi."

"You don't need an alibi. Lenny killed himself."

He was silent for a moment. "I wish people who didn't even know Lenny would stop saying that." He stuck out his chin. "Lenny's mom doesn't think he killed himself. I don't think she's paying you to prove something she doesn't believe."

"I'm sure she'll be satisfied if I can tell her why Lenny did it."

Freddie huffed his disagreement. I lifted the lid to the schoolhouse desk. In the drawer beneath there were Lenny's bills, his bank statements, some time cards, and an address book. I picked up the address book and flipped through it. Mostly first names.

"I'm supposed to be getting ready for a party. It's Bobby's birthday. That's why I thought you might be a present." He paused dramatically. "You know, like in *Boys in the Band*."

"Yeah, I know. It was at The Parkway two months ago." Not that I'd particularly enjoyed it. They were a whiny bunch. But it did prompt me to ask, "How did Lenny feel about being gay?"

"I don't think he thought about it much. He was too busy sucking cock." I suppose it was meant to shock me, but it didn't. "I knew you were gay the minute you walked in," Freddie continued.

"Oh yeah? What gave me away?"

"I'm almost naked. You keep pretending not to notice. Pretend being the operative word."

It's embarrassing, but I'm used to guys flirting with me. I'm six foot three and weigh about two-ten. I work out a few times a week to make sure the scale doesn't tick much higher. That month, my dark hair was just beginning to curl since I needed a haircut. I was thinking about giving a beard a try, or maybe I was just being lazy. Either way, in addition to my mustache, there was heavy stubble all over my face. Trouble, in the form of boys who look like Freddie, always seems to find me. I guess that means I'm good looking.

"Tell me more about Lenny," I asked, ignoring his flirting.

"Lenny wrote poetry. Dreadful poetry. I can show you some if you want, but my guess is Mrs. Borlock isn't paying you enough to actually read it." He pointed to a stack of black and white composition books by Lenny's mattress. I shook my head. I might have to read them sometime, but hopefully I could figure this out without them.

I picked up Lenny's bank statements and flipped through them.

"We're all artsy, the four of us. Bobby is an actor. I'm a painter, a primitive representationalist. I work mostly in acrylics and found objects." He paused, waiting for me to look up at the painting over his bed and compliment it. I stuck to the bank statements, so he continued, "Chuck is in a band called The Wigs. It's glam rock. They all wear makeup and have pretty hair, but Chuck's the only one who's gay. They're touring. Well, I mean they have a gig in Bloomington."

Contrary to what Freddie had said, Lenny wasn't broke. His most recent bank balance was nearly four thousand dollars. I flipped back over the past few months. His previous balances were significantly smaller, usually never more than six or seven hundred at the most. He'd even overdrawn the account a few times. I went back to the most recent statement. Halfway down the page, there was a circled deposit for three thousand, five hundred, and sixty-four dollars.

"Did Lenny come into some money recently?"

"No."

"What did he do for money?"

"Oh, we're all temps. It's very flexible. We work for a service called Carolyn's Crew. Carolyn's great. She used to be an actress, so she understands."

"She give bonuses?"

"Oh, yeah. If you stay on an assignment for two months, you get a hundred dollars. Then two hundred at six months. Lenny was about to get his second bonus."

"Lenny had been on the assignment for a while, then?"

"He was having a rough time of it, though."

"What do you mean a rough time?"

"Well, I'm not sure. He talked about his boss a lot, this guy named Campbell. Obviously, the guy had money. No one names their kid Campbell unless they're also giving him a trust fund. One minute Lenny adored the guy, and the next he hated him. I think Lenny had a crush and it wasn't going well."

"Do you think they might have had a relationship?"

"No, if Lenny was having sex with someone he wouldn't shut up about it. Seriously, I can tell you the size of every dick he's touched for the last two years." He looked at me expectantly, like I might ask him to do so. Curtly, he said, "I'm trying to seduce you, but you seem not to notice."

"I notice."

Freddie watched me, waiting for me to make a move. When I didn't, he padded over to me. Frowning, he looked up and asked, "Are you trying to hurt my feelings?" He was so short I had to practically pick him up to kiss him.

Of course, I knew I shouldn't have sex with him. It wasn't what you'd call a reliable interrogation technique. But he didn't seem to know why Lenny killed himself, didn't even think Lenny did kill himself, so it was hard to see the harm in it.

Pushing me away, Freddie flopped down on the bed and, lifting his hips, slid off his gym shorts. His dick was semi-hard in anticipation and belonged on a much bigger man. I slipped off my jacket and began to undo the underarm holster holding my 9mm Sig Sauer.

"No," Freddie said with a devilish smile. "Leave that on."

I threw my jacket on the floor and joined Freddie on the bed. Taking him into my arms, I kissed him long and deep. There was something sexy about his being completely naked and my having most of my clothes still on. My hard-on rubbed against his, the cotton of my jeans making it all the more exciting. He pulled away from me and looked into my eyes. "You're a good kisser."

I thanked him for the compliment by kissing him some more. His hands were in my jeans, working to unbutton them and set my dick free. Once he got it into the open, he gave an appreciative little growl. He jerked me a few times and then rubbed our cocks together.

"This is going to be so good," he whispered, then rolled over and spooned his naked butt into my lap. I ran my hands across his chest, pinching his nipples. He reached behind himself, grabbing my dick and rubbing the head along the crack of his ass.

His breathing began to come faster, and, somewhat abruptly, he reached around the edge of the mattress and pulled out a small container of Vaseline. Quickly, he lubed up my dick and his pucker hole. Before I slid my dick in, he said, "Take it easy at first."

I fucked him slowly for a bit, lying there on my side with my pants down around my knees, giving him time to relax into it. Soon, though, I became impatient and pushed him over until he was face down. I crawled on top of him and slipped my cock back into him. He groaned happily.

My hands on his hips, I had to splay my legs wide to get a good angle. I thrust into him until the muscles on the insides of my legs began to ache. I pulled my legs closer together and lifted him up with me. His knees were off the bed, his ass practically floating in front of me as I pounded into him. His moaning began to blend into one long keening sound that reminded me of a siren.

Then I flipped him over. I wanted to see the look on his face while I screwed him. When he looked up at me, he stopped moaning and grinned. I slid back into him. "Yeah, that's it," he whispered.

Taking his cock into my hand, I started to jack him off. Matching each stroke with a thrust. He pushed my hand away. "You're going to make me come too soon."

I wanted to make him come, though, so I fucked him harder and faster. My holstered gun bounced against my ribs. He arched his hips, meeting each thrust. His hard cock bounced on his belly, and then he was coming. I reached out and jerked him a few times to help him along. All the while, I kept fucking him.

When he stopped spasming, Freddie said, "Pull it out. I want to see you come."

I pulled out of him and began to jack myself off. It only took a few pumps and I was coming all over Freddie's reddened dick and his already sticky belly. I collapsed on top of him. He slipped his arms around me and squeezed me close.

When he'd caught his breath, he said, "I hope this means you'll try extra hard to find out what happened to Lenny."

I pulled away from him, "Is that what this is about? You fucked me so I'd do a good job?"

"No, I fucked you because you're sexy. But I can still ask for special treatment, can't I?"

"I always do a good job," I said.

He shrugged. "You never asked for my alibi."

"Okay, tell me your alibi." Obviously, he was eager to do so.

"The night before Lenny died, I got drunk off my ass on Long Island Iced Teas and took the bus in the wrong direction! This big, burly black guy took pity on me. After that, all I remember is holding onto a bathroom sink in some apartment while the black guy fucked the living daylights out of me. I woke up the next morning around eleven. I had no idea where I was." He watched me to see what kind of reaction his story might get.

I didn't know what the big deal was with his alibi. Was he that desperate to display his sexual prowess? Did he want to present himself as some kind of slut? Was this his way of saying, "don't take what we just did too seriously"?

I dead-panned it. "Could you find this guy again?"

"Probably not."

"Then it's not an alibi, is it?"

He frowned. "Oh. I guess not."

I rolled over and looked at him. "Can you think of anything else that might be important?"

Freddie thought for a moment, then smiled. "He would have liked you. That's for sure. You're just his type."

It was time for me to leave, so I got off the bed. My hands and cock were still gooey with Vaseline. "Which way is the bathroom?"

"It's right across the hall."

With my pants around my ankles, I had to waddle across the hall. When I got halfway to the john, the front door opened and in walked Bobby Martin. Immediately, I remembered him. I'd picked him up at The Loading Zone a couple months before. I never saw him after that. We hadn't exchanged numbers.

He took a moment to look me up and down. My greasy shirttails, my red, sticky cock hanging out, my hairy knees. He smiled and said, "Well, nice to see you again."

I wanted to punch someone.

# # #

The next morning it was raining in a way that reminded me of Noah and his ark. I walked out of my apartment and decided to take a cab. I'd been cursing myself for my behavior at Lenny's apartment for nearly twenty-four hours, and promised myself I'd get this case back on a professional level.

At some point I was going to have to interview Bobby Martin. I'd declined to do it the day before. It would have been more convenient, of course, but when interviewing a subject you should at least have the illusion of the upper hand. This is natural for a police officer, but for a private investigator it's harder to establish, and as a private investigator caught with his pants down it's all but impossible. I promised myself I'd get back to him soon.

The station for the eighteenth district was on Chicago Avenue; it was three stories, brick, and had a Gothic-looking, white granite façade. I jumped out of the cab and ran into the building. I'd called around and found out that a Detective Harker had handled the Borlock case. The sergeant at the front desk told me he was located on the third floor.

When I got to the third floor, I found that most of the floor was devoted to one big room with desks spread around it. Four-drawer file cabinets created wall-like barriers between some of the desks. Harker's desk was in the back corner, hiding behind a couple file cabinets.

Detective Bert Harker was forty-something, about five seven, had a blond crew cut and a nose that was bent at the bridge, making his profile look like the Indian on the flipside of a buffalo nickel. When he looked up at me, I could see that his eyes were a washed-out blue. The aviator-style glasses he wore made them seem just a little too big. He wore a rumpled, tan suit with a white shirt and a dark tie. Underneath, his body looked to be wiry and tense, like he was poised to spring at any moment.

"Detective Harker?" I asked.

"Yeah?"

"I'm Nick Nowak. I'm a private—"

"I know who you are."

Most of my family was on the job, plus I'd been a cop myself for about six years and left under a kind of cloud. The fact that he knew me wasn't a good thing. "I've been hired by Helen Borlock to look into her son's death."

"Suicide," he corrected.

"Mrs. Borlock says he was a pretty happy kid."

Harker shrugged. "She's his mother. What else is she gonna say?"

"I talked to one of his roommates. He said pretty much the same thing."

"Yeah, well, his boss, Campbell Wayne, said Lenny seemed depressed. Mentioned he was having problems with his roommates. Said he showed up a couple times like he was on something."

This was new, and exactly the kind of thing I needed to know. "You wanna tell me about Campbell Wayne?"

"Vice President of Marketing at JTM Properties, located on the forty-second floor of the Hancock. Too slick for my taste, but I have no reason to doubt what he said."

"What else do you have?"

"You wanna see the file?" he asked.

I figured he was taunting me. "Don't pull my leg, okay?"

"If I pull your leg, you'll know it." If he hadn't said it in such an expressionless way, I might have thought he was flirting. Without missing a beat, he continued, "It's not an active investigation. And we'd all like Mrs. Borlock to stop calling. When you figure out this is a suicide, which you will, you'll get Mrs. Borlock to leave us alone. Deal?"

I nodded. "I'll make sure she understands."

Harker walked over to a filing cabinet and dug around for the file. When he found it, he looked around the big room and said, "Come on." He led me back to a small interview room with just a table, a metal ashtray, and a couple chairs. He tossed the file onto the table. It was manila, about an eighth of an inch thick. I thought that was pretty sad. A guy's life and death reduced to an eighth of an inch.

I pulled up a chair while Harker leaned against a wall. Even though there wasn't much in the file, I took a pad out of my jacket pocket and got ready to take some notes. I lit a cigarette so I could concentrate. There was an autopsy report that counted up exactly how many bones Lenny broke falling from the seventh floor to land next to a flower stand on the first. It noted that some blood had been sent for a toxicology report, but that report wasn't in the file—probably hadn't come back yet. There were witness statements from the florist on the first floor and a customer she was waiting on; neither of whom saw anything until Lenny had already hit the marble floor about ten feet from where they stood.

The whole time I was reading the file, Harker watched me. It began to bug me, so I said, "You stay in here much longer and the whole district is gonna think you're getting a blow job."

He stared at me a moment, then said, "And if I leave you alone with my file, half of it walks away in your pocket."

I couldn't deny that, so I went back to studying the file. The most important thing in it was the witness statement from Jeanine Anderson, a hostess at The Gold Mine, a high-end hamburger chain with a gold rush theme. She was setting up her station when she noticed Lenny lingering around the spot he eventually jumped from. She said he was alone and that he looked sad. I jotted down her name and the gist of her statement.

According to the detective's report, it was determined that Lenny must have jumped from a spot between twelve and fifteen feet north of the elevator. I made a note to check that out. I looked over the statement from Campbell Wayne. It said the things Harker had told me. It also said that Lenny was a good worker, conscientious and detail-oriented. He was punctual and sometimes wrote poetry at his desk during lunch. On the day Lenny died, he'd arrived on time and gone for a coffee break about ten o'clock. They noticed he hadn't come back, but it wasn't until several hours later that they heard he'd gone next door to Water Tower and jumped.

"Why go to work at all?"

The comment was more to myself, but Harker answered, "Maybe he didn't decide to do it until he got there."

"I suppose. But slitting your wrists in a nice warm bath seems cozier." Did it, though? One of his roommates would have found him. And they'd have had to clean up the mess. Maybe this was the most considerate way he could think to do it.

"I heard about you, you know," Harker said. "About what happened."

I closed the file. I'd gotten pretty much everything I could out of it.

"Yeah, what did you hear?" I asked. If he was subtly trying to call me a fag, I wasn't going to stand for it. I'd rather he come right out and say it.

"I heard you and your boyfriend got jumped." After a long pause, he asked, "How's he doing?"

Suddenly, I couldn't really breathe. I don't know whether it was because he was talking about my ex, a subject that always messed with my head, or whether the fact that he was a cop and he was maybe being nice about the whole thing was scaring the shit out of me.

"I don't know how he's doing. We don't talk," I managed to say.

He nodded like he knew this was always the outcome when two gay lovers got beaten up by four suburban teenagers. We exchanged business cards, and I hurried out of the station like everyone in it had an infectious disease.

# # #

When I got back to my office, I looked up the number for JTM Properties and put in a call to Campbell Wayne. It was about ten-forty-five. A man answered the phone.

"Campbell Wayne, please," I said.

"Who's calling?" he asked. Obviously, he was a temp like Lenny. I told him who I was and why I was calling. "Just a moment."

He put me on hold. I listened to the silence for about two minutes, then he was back on the line. "Mr. Wayne is not available at the moment. Can I have him call you?"

I left my number.

I spent the rest of the day doing background checks for a brokerage firm that kicks me a steady amount of work. They've got offices all over the country and a surprising number of people with access to cash accounts. I check for felonies, extra names, and general bad behavior. I suggest they *not* hire about ten percent of the people whose names they send. Presumably, they take my suggestions.

At five-fifteen, Campbell Wayne still hadn't called me back. That was a problem. It was also a problem that I'd smoked an entire pack of cigarettes since lunch. Something was bugging me. I hoped it was Campbell Wayne and the Borlock case.

There were a couple things about the case that could be getting to me. One was the money I found in Lenny's bank account. That required an explanation. I know rich people kill themselves all the time, but a kid who's normally broke and then comes into some money...well, it seemed like he'd at least spend the money first.

The other thing was that there was something wrong about Wayne saying Lenny was depressed and Freddie saying he was happy. One of them was lying. My gut, and the fact that he hadn't called back, was telling me the liar was Campbell Wayne. Of course, I had to be careful not to discount the possibility that Freddie was lying his head off.

I couldn't let the fact that I'd recently fucked him cloud my vision.

Before I zeroed in on this Wayne guy, I'd need to do more checking. Or at least talk to him.

Unfortunately, the Borlock case wasn't what was bugging me, and I knew it. I was bugged about my ex, Daniel. Whenever someone brought him up, the way Harker did, the idea of him floated around me like a dark cloud for a day or two. Harker had asked me how Daniel was. I had no idea, and, to be honest, I'd like to know. We'd ended abruptly and hadn't talked since. He even moved his stuff out of our apartment while I was at work. After nearly two years, I still hadn't filled in the empty spots he left in my living room.

When I met Daniel, I'd been with the Chicago Police Department about three years. After high school, I floated around doing odd jobs. I pulled high numbers in the draft lottery three years in a row, so that wasn't a problem. Yes, there was flak about this in my family. They're a pretty anti-commie bunch, but they calmed down when I signed up for the Training Academy.

I'd been dating women on and off, hoping that if I just got close enough something would click. It didn't. I met Daniel's sister, Donna, at a bar on Rush and dated her half a dozen times over the course of two months. She probably thought I was an alcoholic, since I claimed to be too drunk twice to avoid sex. Even though it wasn't going so well, at least in the sex department, she invited me to a family outing.

It was summer, and Donna's family had turned out in force at some park up near Evanston. Her grandmother was turning eighty, and to most of their family that seemed a good reason to stand in the sun and drink beer while the kids ate too much cake and screamed their heads off.

Daniel showed up in a pair of roller skates, tube socks with bright blue stripes, a pair of frayed cut-offs, and a tank top that had an angel printed on it. He was small, tightly muscled, naturally blond, and had eyes that were sometimes gray and sometimes blue. That day I had to be careful not to spend too much time looking at him.

At twenty-four, Daniel was finishing up a graduate degree in library sciences. Out of the blue, he called me and said he needed to talk to me. I invited him to the studio apartment I had near Lincoln Park. When he showed up, he told me that Donna had begun to date someone else. And when I didn't get too upset, he made a pass at me. With Daniel I didn't have to make any excuses, and we moved into our apartment on Roscoe six weeks later.

I still live in the Roscoe apartment. The building is three stories, brick, and shaped like a sort of W, with two wings that come out to meet the street and a stunted wing that juts out from the center partway into the courtyard. I live in the garden apartment at the front of the eastern wing.

When I got home that night, I was soaked from taking a bus in the rain. I would have cabbed it, but the expense was getting to me. I stripped off my clothes and took a hot shower. I tried to jack off while I was in there, figuring that might be the itch that needed scratching, but it just wasn't happening.

I put on a pair of sweats and an old rugby shirt. The phone was in the living room, so I went out there and sat in one of my director's chairs that faced the spot where a sofa had once been. I'd had his phone number for more than a year. He was listed, so getting it wasn't exactly detective work. Every once in a while I dialed six of the seven numbers, then hung up. For some reason, that night I dialed the seventh number.

I nearly hung up while it rang, but then he picked up. "Hello?" His voice seemed small and very far away.

"It's me."

Static, then he said, "I thought you'd call. Eventually."

"Yeah, well...how are you?"

"Groggy. I got out of the hospital a couple days ago. I'm still on pain medication."

"Your eye?"

"Cheekbone reconstruction. It's the last one. I don't really want to talk about it." I didn't want to talk about it, either, to be truthful. My boyfriend getting hit in the face with a baseball bat while I stood around watching wasn't the kind of thing that made me chatty.

"I'm not a cop anymore."

"I know. I heard. You're like a private eye?"

It bothered me that he knew more about me than I knew about him. "Yeah, I'm a private investigator."

We were silent long enough for it to become uncomfortable.

"Well..." he said.

"Are you seeing anyone?" I asked.

"I was. Didn't work out. You?"

"No one that matters." I replied. Rashly, I told him, "I miss you."

"That isn't what I want to hear."

"What do you want to hear?"

"If I tell you, it won't mean anything."

# # #

Friday morning it drizzled. Umbrella in hand, I walked out to Lake Shore and caught an express bus down to Michigan Avenue. I hopped off at the second stop and made my way over to Water Tower Place. It was just about ten o'clock when I walked into the mall. I headed across the beige marble floor to the glass elevator. The basic shape of the place was octagonal. When the elevator arrived, I hit seven and turned around to watch the mall pass by as the elevator climbed.

The mall was actually eight levels: a ground level, a mezzanine level, and then floors two through seven. As I rose in the elevator, I watched the stores go by. Lord & Taylor, Marshall Field's, Florsheim, Waldenbooks, Chess King, some boutiques trying to get started, a Musicland. At the seventh floor, I got out and looked around. It was quiet. There weren't any other customers milling about yet. The elevator was on the south side of the octagon. I walked north until I got to the spot where Lenny had jumped.

The reason to pick the seventh floor over, say, the fifth or the fourth, is that while the octagonal openings get bigger and bigger for the other floors, the top two floors actually get smaller. If you tried jumping off the fifth floor, you'd end up on the fourth, and while you might have hurt yourself pretty bad, you probably wouldn't be very dead. Jumping from the seventh was pretty much a guarantee.

Regardless of whether it was suicide or murder, some thought had been given to Lenny's death ahead of time. Standing in the spot where Lenny jumped, I looked around. What was he thinking about? Did he think, "Wow, the last thing I'm going to see in my life is a Kroch's & Brentano's?" Or was he in so much emotional pain he couldn't think, could only focus on forcing himself to jump?

Not too long ago, I watched someone commit suicide by jumping. The part that was most disturbing was how prosaic it looked. One minute the guy was standing there, the next he was gone. That's what it would have looked like with Lenny. He would have been walking around looking down the atrium, just like everyone does. Then he would have climbed over the railing, calmly, like he was climbing over the fence in someone's backyard.

Even in my darkest moments, after Daniel and I broke up and I left my job with the Chicago Police Department, suicide hadn't crossed my mind. I was in a lot of pain, and I suppose if the pain had been worse, or if I had a lower threshold for it, I might have considered suicide. Just as a way to make the pain go away, maybe. I wondered if that had happened with Lenny. Was he in that much pain? Had something gone that wrong with his life? If I could find the source of his pain, it would put Mrs. Borlock's mind at ease. Or at least I hoped it would.

To be thorough, I spent a few minutes considering the possibility that he hadn't killed himself. If he didn't jump, then someone had to have pushed him. Except the octagon was circled in thick glass about four and a half feet high, with a large chrome tube running around the edge of the railing. No one could push you over. They'd have to lift you. If someone lifted Lenny and tilted him over the edge, he'd have to be bigger than Lenny. I realized I didn't know how tall Lenny was. I pulled out my note pad and jotted myself a reminder to find out.

So, to get him over the edge, someone had to lift and push at the same time. Lenny would have been trying to break free, trying to prevent himself from going over, but there wouldn't have been anything to grab onto to stop his fall. The chrome tube wouldn't have been any help at all; he wouldn't have been able to get any purchase. No, the only thing to grab on to was whoever was doing the lifting. I put myself in Lenny's position and tried to think it through. If I was expecting it, I would have grabbed for the killer. And if I grabbed for the killer, I might have scratched him. I made note to ask Detective Harker if he noticed any scratches on anyone he talked to.

I wandered around the seventh floor for a few minutes. There was a high-end women's boutique, a Rose Records, a shop that sold crystal and leaded glass, and a pair of escalators that took you down to the sixth floor. Tucked in a corner was a men's room. I popped in.

It was large and empty. Everything was marble like the rest of the mall. There were five stalls. I walked to the farthest one from the door and opened it. I studied the walls. The outer two walls were marble, the inner ones beige-painted metal. It was clean. They really paid attention here. Graffiti wouldn't last long.

However, next to the toilet paper dispenser, scratched into the paint, was the quaint little invitation "BJ 3:00 Thurs." Obviously, Lenny hadn't responded to that invitation, but I wondered if there might have been another, one written in pen that had later been cleaned off? Or, more likely, did Lenny just think the restroom was cruisy and come over to check it out during his coffee break? Did he make a pass at the wrong guy? The kind of guy who wouldn't worry too much about tossing a fag off the seventh floor? It was a possibility I couldn't discount.

I walked out of the men's room and circled the floor again. It was time to check out the witness, Jeanine Anderson. The Gold Mine was a theme restaurant where they served expensive, half-pound burgers with clever names like The Prospector and The Motherlode. You had to enter the dark restaurant through a long mineshaft. The hostess station was three quarters of the way down the twisting shaft.

As I walked by, I noticed a pretty young woman setting up the station. Figuring it must be Jeanine, I walked over. "Hi, are you Jeanine?" I asked. I didn't really know what I was going to say next, but it probably wouldn't be the truth.

"No, Jeanine doesn't work on Fridays." She said this as though Jeanine wasn't quite good enough to work Fridays. She flicked her long hair over her shoulder.

"When is she here?"

"Are you a friend of hers?" She narrowed her eyes at me. This girl was pretty enough to have had trouble with guys; obviously she figured that's what this was.

"You know what, I'll just call her at home." I hoped that this girl would figure I was a good friend and not even bother to mention it to Jeanine.

When I turned around, I knew something was wrong. Looking down the mineshaft, all I could see was the entrance to the glass elevator and part of the crystal store. Jeanine's statement had to be wrong. She specifically said she'd seen Lenny hanging around the spot where he jumped. From the hostess station, the only place she could have seen him hanging around was the elevator.

I turned around and asked today's hostess one more question. "Is this where the hostess stand always is? Or do you move it further up?"

She gave me a quizzical look. "What kind of question is that? Are you some kind of inspector? Do I need to get the manager?"

I told her to have a nice day and left.

On the first floor, I found a payphone. I called Campbell Wayne's office and asked for him. He still couldn't come to the phone. "Actually, I'd like to make an appointment with him. Can you take care of that?" I asked.

The temp put me back on hold. He was gone a long time. I was beginning to think I should have brought a book when he came back on the line. "Mr. Wayne's schedule is very full, and he feels that since he's already spoken to the police there wouldn't be much point."

Somehow I wasn't surprised.

"All right. I'll give you a call tomorrow and see if his schedule has loosened up," I said, because I knew he'd repeat it to Mr. Wayne.

After I hung up, I stood there stewing. I could try ambushing the executive, but I figured as soon as I identified myself he'd clam up. I had an idea; it was a little crazy, but it seemed like the only way I'd get to talk to Campbell Wayne. I picked up the payphone again and called Bobby Martin. I told him my idea, and he giggled, but agreed to help. He had a phone call or two to make, but said he'd meet me at the bagel place on Oak Street around lunchtime.

# # #

Bobby walked into Nosh wearing a bright yellow raincoat he'd obviously gotten at a thrift store. The rain had probably stopped before he left his apartment, but he was likely too thrilled by the opportunity to wear his raincoat to notice. I took a good look at him as he waited at the counter. His hair was a sandy color, trimmed in the back and over his ears, but allowed to grow long in the front. You couldn't tell it, but beneath his raincoat he had a tight little body and a nice fat ass.

After he got coffee and a sesame bagel, he caught me up on all the doings in his life. He told me all about his acting class, several auditions he'd been on for plays he wasn't cast in, hinted that he'd been having lots of really great sex, and complained about what a little bitch Freddie could be. Then he said, "Well, that's all that's new with me. How about you?"

"You left out the part where Lenny died."

He looked away, blinked a few times. "Oh, I almost forgot. I finally bought Blondie's new album. I know it's been out—"

"Stop it," I told him. We sat quietly for a few moments.

"I talk too much when I'm nervous."

"No kidding," I said. "How did you find me? We didn't exchange numbers."

"You're not the only one who can detect things." I waited. "I went back to your apartment and got your name from the mail box. Then I looked in the phone book under private investigator. It wasn't rocket science."

I almost asked, "Why me?" but that was pretty obvious. A straight private investigator might not have given Lenny much more attention than the police. And there probably weren't many other private investigators Bobby had slept with.

"I need to ask you a few things about Lenny." After my walk around Water Tower, there were some things I should try to clear up, and Bobby was probably the person to do it. He waited. "How tall was Lenny?"

"Not tall. Five seven maybe. Why?"

I ignored his question, thinking instead that at five seven there were a lot of men big enough to throw Lenny off the seventh floor of Water Tower Place. "Did he talk about his sex life with you?"

"Of course, we were sisters."

"Was he likely to pick someone up in a restroom?"

Bobby gave this some thought. "He never told me about anything like that. Lenny liked to be adventurous, though, so... maybe. The thing is, though, he liked to get fucked, and I can imagine him giving someone a quick hand job or even sucking a guy off, but getting fucked in a mall men's room? That seems a bit...elaborate."

I nodded. It made sense. Lenny being killed by a pickup was still a possibility, but a more remote one.

"What do you know about Campbell Wayne?"

"Lenny thought he was like a character in a movie. Good looking, great dresser, charming. He's dating the boss' daughter. I couldn't tell you whether it's the J, the T, or the M. But it's one of them. Lenny was always doing things like making reservations at the trendiest restaurants, responding to charity events and art openings. I think the guy was even on the society page a couple of times."

"Do you think he and Lenny had something going on?"

Bobby shook his head. "Lenny thought he was a closet case, but he thinks that about everyone." He frowned at his mistake in tense, but didn't correct himself.

"Freddie said you and he used to be boyfriends."

"For about five minutes. I love him dearly, but we're not what you'd call sexually compatible." He studied me for a moment, then burst out laughing. "You don't think Freddie had something to do with Lenny's death?"

Actually, I didn't. Freddie was far too short to throw Lenny over the railing at Water Tower. He'd need to have brought a stepladder. Still, I didn't like loose ends. I told him, "Sometimes it's my job to ask stupid questions."

Bobby looked at his watch. "We should get going. Our appointment is at one."

Carolyn's Crew Temporary Agency was located on the second floor of a small office building on Superior. Basically it was one large office with two desks and a half dozen filing cabinets on one wall. Each of the desks had a large, elaborate phone with multiple lines. The larger desk was arranged by the window and belonged to the owner, Carolyn O'Hara. Every available wall surface was covered with framed eight-by-tens from the actors she'd gotten temp jobs for.

When we walked in, both Carolyn and her secretary were on the phone. Bobby led me over to a couple of chairs sitting in front of Carolyn's desk. I took a good look at her while she finished her call. She was in her mid-forties. Clearly she'd been a beauty when she was young; her bones were strong, and she was still handsome. Her hair was dyed a flaming red, and her make-up was too heavy for fluorescent lighting. She wore a silky, wrap-around dress that would have made a splash at any disco five years ago.

Setting down the phone, she looked at us expectantly. Bobby introduced me, and she gave me an appraising look. "Bobby told me what you'd like to do, but I'm not sure. I could lose a client if you're found out. I could lose a lot of clients. A lot of people rely on me."

That's when I noticed Carolyn's eight-by-ten in the crowd of actors above the window. The photo looked to be about ten years old. I nodded. She was right; a lot of people did rely on her.

"Bobby recommended me to you, and you sent me out on an assignment to give me a try. Nobody needs to know more than that."

She thought about it for a moment. "I don't think anyone will believe it. I wouldn't." She sighed heavily. "If I was smart, I'd call my lawyer and get his opinion."

"If you want to do that, I understand."

"Lenny made me laugh every time I talked to him. I think that's all that really matters. Do you type, at least?"

"Yes," I told her. I'd taken typing in high school. Police work requires a lot of paperwork, much of it typed. Private investigation is even worse. My skills weren't too bad.

"Okay. I'm going to give you a typing test and have you fill out an application, just to keep things official. On the application, I'd appreciate it if you don't put down anything I could actually check. I don't think this is illegal, but I could probably get myself sued."

I nodded. She led me to a tiny room, which was really just a closet, where there was a small table with an IBM Selectric on it. Bobby squeezed in with me, and we began to make up names for companies I'd previously worked for. Most importantly, I had to make up a name. I'd left my name with Campbell Wayne's temp. He might not remember it, but I couldn't take that chance.

"Lance," Bobby suggested. "You look like a Lance."

"I don't think so. Ted," I said as I wrote in on the application. Theodore was Daniel's middle name. I didn't explain that to Bobby.

"Ted what?" he asked. "Jones?"

"Duda," I said.

"Oh, that's ridiculous," exclaimed Bobby.

"It's not ridiculous, it's Polish. It's my mother's maiden name. If I show up as Lance Lamour, it will be a little suspicious. Don't you think?"

Bobby shrugged in defeat.

When I finished the typing test, Bobby and I went back to Carolyn's desk. She glanced at the application. "Nice to meet you, Ted Duda. You need to work on your typing. You scored forty-five words a minute, but your accuracy is not good. Fortunately, he's asked for light typing. You start on Monday. I had Shelly call Brice and tell him another client requested him. Had to give him a twenty-five-cent raise to make it sound legit." She eyed me like that part was my fault.

Something occurred too me. "You always send a guy. Don't most offices prefer women for secretarial work?"

"They do. It's not exactly legal, but that doesn't stop them from asking. To be honest, I'd rather not send my people anywhere they might not be comfortable. It's a temp job, not a crusade."

"So why does Wayne ask for a guy?"

"His fiancée. He says she's the jealous type."

# # #

That evening when I got home, I spent about twenty minutes wandering around my neighborhood looking for my car. Other than moving my car from parking space to parking space, I hadn't really used it in about two weeks. So its location wasn't exactly fresh in my mind. I finally found it on Elaine Place.

The winter had taken a toll on my 1974 Plymouth Duster. Rust had continued to devour the baby blue paint job, and there were several spots where I could see right through my side panels. Another winter and I might not have fenders at all.

There had been a thick layer of heavy gray clouds all day, but so far it hadn't rained a drop. Now that the sun had set, it was a dark, starless night. As I headed out to Niles, I could have taken the expressway, but it seemed more trouble than it was worth. Instead, I went up Lincoln

Avenue until I got to Touhy and took that into the suburb. The Borlocks lived in a small, modest neighborhood. Their house was a two-bedroom brick ranch on an eighth of an acre.

As I pulled into the driveway, Helen opened up the screen door and came out onto the stoop. She had a tea towel in her hand, as though she'd just been washing dishes. She greeted me like I was a family friend and ushered me into the living room. Mr. Borlock sat in a brown Naugahyde recliner watching a show with Robert Wagner and a redhead. I'd heard of the show before, but couldn't remember its name. It's the one about a rich couple who get so bored, they solve crimes.

Helen introduced me to her husband, but he never looked up. "Don't pay any attention to him," she said. She sat me down at her colonial dining table and asked, "Do you like beer?"

"I'm fine, thanks."

"But do you *like* beer?"

"Yeah, I do."

"Good. You're having one."

She went around the corner into the tiny kitchen, I heard the refrigerator pop open, and a moment later Helen came back with two glasses and two cans of beer. She poured them out and pushed one in my direction. Then she sat down in a chair and eagerly pulled it up to the table. "So, what have you found out?"

I wished I'd had time to type up a report for her and reminded myself to take care of that over the weekend. "I've met with Lenny's roommates, Bobby and Freddie.

They agree with you that Lenny wasn't showing any outward signs of depression."

She nodded, happy they agreed with her, although she probably knew that already.

"I visited the detective in charge of the case, and he was nice enough to let me look at the file. He didn't have to do that. He's hoping that I'll agree with him that it's suicide and get you to stop calling them."

"But you aren't going to agree with him," she asserted.

"There are some things I'm uncomfortable with, but that doesn't mean it won't eventually turn out to be suicide," I explained as honestly as I could.

She frowned.

"Are you sure this is going to make you feel better? I mean, even if someone did hurt Lenny. He's still gone. Nothing really changes." I felt I had to say this. I couldn't keep taking her money if she had unreasonable expectations about what the result might be.

She took a deep breath and then let it go.

"My son was twenty-three years old. It's a terrible thing to die that young. But Lenny...he was a happy child, a funny man, always smiling. Always wanting to make other people smile. He made up jokes for me, ever since he was a child. Terrible jokes. Stupid, really. And that made them funnier in a way. I'd always laugh at them. I think he had more happiness in his twenty-three years than most people have in eighty. If he killed himself...that means he was in pain. Probably for a very long time, and I didn't know. I'm his mother, and I didn't know. I'm not sure I can bear that."

We sat there for a few moments. Sipped our beers. The TV in the other room played a commercial for the Buick Regal.

"There's a curious deposit in Lenny's bank account. It's for three thousand, five hundred, and sixty-four dollars. Does that make sense to you?"

"No. It doesn't make any sense." She lowered her voice. "Last year, Lenny got into some money trouble, and his father gave him five hundred dollars. Every month for the last six months, he'd give his father twenty-five dollars. If he had that kind of money, he'd have paid his father back. With interest."

I nodded. There was definitely something wrong about the deposit.

"The man Lenny was temping for has refused to take my calls or see me," I told her. "It seems suspicious, but it could be nothing."

"No, I think it's very suspicious."

"I've arranged with Lenny's temp agency to send me there and work the same assignment Lenny had."

Helen's eyes grew large. "You're going undercover?"

"Only if you approve. I'm hoping—"

"I approve!" Helen said.

"Okay, just wait a moment. I'm hoping it will take a week or less to get the information I need. However, it might take longer. It might also be a dead end. Just because someone's uncooperative, doesn't mean they're guilty."

She smiled. "Your plan is just like on *Charlie's Angels*. Lenny would like that. He loved that show."

# # #

Saturday morning, I woke up being nuzzled by Ross, my friend, co-worker, and frequent bedmate. We worked together at Paradise Isle, a disco where I manned the door on Friday and Saturday nights and he bartended five nights a week. Or, rather, where I used to man the door and Ross used to work. It burned down on Valentine's Day.

Ross and I had a habit of getting together after work on Friday or Saturday nights, since his boyfriend was likely to be with the wife and kids in Naperville. Even without work, the habit had continued. Ross smelled like sleep and sweat and stale beer, so I couldn't resist when he whispered, "Fuck me," in my ear.

A lot of guys came to Paradise Isle just to watch Ross work. Like the other bartenders, he spent much of the night shirtless. Uniformly, they all had well-defined chests and bulging biceps. What Ross had that they didn't was a disarming, boyish charm. He had freckles sprinkled across his nose and onto his cheeks, and a cowlick on the left just at his hairline.

We kissed deeply, and I held both our dicks in my hand. Mine was longer and thicker, while his curved out away from his body at the top. Ross was largely a top, and I'd only fucked him one or two times. Usually when we got together, he'd blow me or we'd jack each other off. My gut said his request meant something was up, but I put off worrying about it until later.

He wrapped his legs around me and whispered, "I want you in me, now." I scrambled for the Vaseline and got us both ready. He grimaced a bit when I entered him. His ass was tight and clamped down on my dick. I kissed him around the neck and whispered, "Relax," into his ear.

He closed his eyes, and I kissed his eyelids. Slowly, I moved inside of him. Pulling my hips back a bit, then pushing them forward. His breathing caught each time I pushed.

Ross liked dirty talk. "You want me to fuck you hard?" I asked.

"Yeah, fuck me hard."

"You're sure?" I teased.

"Just do it."

I started fucking him hard and fast. "Oh God!" he gasped.

Holding him by the ankles, I plowed into him again and again. He encouraged me by saying, "Harder, harder..." over and over again. His fist pounding his cock, Ross' face squeezed together. His toes curled. I knew he was getting close.

Teasingly, I came to a complete stop. He let out a whine and wiggled his hips in frustration. I chuckled, then pulled back as far as I could without popping out and slammed back into him. He gasped. I did it a few more times, picking up speed each time. Just as I was getting back to speed, Ross came in three heavy spurts. A couple more thrusts and I came deep inside him.

A lot of guys find sex a great sleep aid and are ready to nod off the minute they're done. I'm the opposite. It energizes me, makes me want to start my day. As I lay there with Ross, he dozed in my arms while I worked over the Borlock case in my mind.

Bobby had mentioned that Campbell Wayne was hobnobbing with the Chicago elite and sometimes landed on the society page. Ross' boyfriend was Earl Silver, the social columnist for the *Daily Herald*. I nudged Ross. "Do you think you could ask Earl about someone involved in a case I'm working?"

He rolled over and stretched. "I'm not sure. I can try, but you're not very popular with Earl."

"He knows about this?"

"Yeah."

"He doesn't think you're going to be faithful, does he? Not while he fucks his wife every weekend."

"He doesn't fuck her."

"Where did the children come from?"

He gave me a nasty look and said, "He doesn't fuck her anymore." He got out of bed and looked around on the floor for his underwear. When he found them, he looked over at me and said, "Actually, things are changing. I'm not going to be able to do this anymore."

That stung. A little more than I would have expected. It also explained why he wanted to get fucked. It was a goodbye gesture. I played it cool and said, "Suit yourself."

"Earl is leaving his wife. They're talking about it tonight. We're going to live together full time."

"Congratulations."

"He's even thinking of coming out. I don't think he'll go that far. But at least he's thinking about it." Ross looked uncomfortable for a moment, like he was afraid I might start a fight with him. "What is it you want me to ask him?"

I gave him Campbell Wayne's name and told him, "What I'm really interested in is the stuff Earl can't print."

Before he left, I stood with Ross at my front door. "Do I get my coat back, at least?" I asked about the gray wool coat he was wearing, which a few months before had been mine.

"I need something to remember you by."

"You can have something to remember me by any time you want to come by."

He frowned, but kissed me goodbye anyway.

After Ross took off, I sat down at the tiny table in my kitchen and cleaned my Sig Sauer. It didn't need it, and I should have been doing laundry, since my first day as a temp was Monday and I'd need something to wear. But I found cleaning my gun to be a calming ritual.

A number of things made me nervous about taking over Lenny's job. Not the least of them was that I wouldn't have my gun with me. An office situation was too risky for an underarm holster. Even if I left my jacket on the whole time—which would likely draw unwanted attention—people might notice the awkward lump under my arm in the harsh fluorescent light of an office.

With an old toothbrush, I cleaned the slide. It had been a long time since I'd been without my gun. Since the time Daniel and I got attacked, I'd pretty much done everything but shower while wearing my holstered Sig Sauer. I was self-aware enough to see the connection, not that I was willing to do much about it. I told myself it was likely that, going into an office every day for a week or so, I probably wouldn't need to shoot anyone. I wished I could take more comfort in that.

I slid a scrap of cloth through the chamber with a dismantled wire coat hanger. Something else wasn't sitting right with me. Ross' news had bummed me out. I had to be honest with myself and admit that. I was fond of Ross, but it didn't go beyond that. I'd miss my fuck buddy, but didn't expect to pine for him.

So it was a bit of a surprise when I realized the thing that was bothering me was Ross dumping me to be with his lover. I was jealous of that, jealous that he had someone, even if it was someone like Earl Silver.

It was a shitty feeling.

# # #

Monday morning, I woke up at four a.m. realizing that I couldn't do it. I couldn't walk around Chicago without my gun. The idea alone made me break out in a cold sweat. I got out of bed and pulled a brown corduroy blazer out of my closet. I grabbed a pair of scissors, an old pillowcase, and a travel sewing kit. It took almost an hour, and the results were downright ugly, but I managed to expand the inside breast pocket of the blazer in such a way that the Sig Sauer would fit. It wouldn't be easy to get to, but if I needed it, it would be nearby.

A few minutes before nine, I walked into JTM pretending to be Ted Duda. I wore the blazer, a rumpled pair of khakis, a dress shirt I'd had to wash twice to get rid of the accumulated dust from two years in my closet, and a red tie my mother had given me when I graduated from high school.

Part of me was nervous that I'd be stopped and asked for identification I didn't have. But Bobby had told me that you could waltz into any building downtown claim you came from a temp agency, pop out an employee's name, and most companies will let you in. When it turned out he was exactly right and I breezed into JTM, I filed the information for later use. It's just the kind of thing that would come in handy in my line of work.

JTM Properties took up half of the forty-second floor of the John Hancock Tower. I had no idea what the company did, though it seemed to have something to do with real estate. The receptionist pointed me toward Campbell Wayne's office, and I wandered across the floor in the general direction she'd pointed. The offices looked hastily put together out of odds and ends. I wondered if the business was fly by night. But then that didn't seem to fit. Why would they have their offices in the Hancock if they were fly by night?

Campbell Wayne's office was tucked in the back, near the northwest corner. One of the diagonal bars that form the Xs on the tower slashed across his window. There was a polished mahogany desk and a leather couch pushed up against a wall. The man himself wasn't in. Outside his office was a dark wooden cubicle that was clearly for me. Around the cubicle and even in Campbell's office were boxes of brochures. I was tempted to rifle through the desk and the surrounding areas to see if Lenny might have left anything interesting, but I thought it might be suspicious behavior, since I'd only just arrived.

I did poke around a little, taking a brochure out of one the boxes. The cover proclaimed "JTM IV" in big letters over a photograph of an office building. Flipping through, there were a lot of charts with dollar amounts and several pages of tiny legalese at the back. The best I could figure, they sold limited partnerships in commercial real estate. One whole section of the brochure was devoted to potential tax benefits. In other words, immediate losses you could deduct from your taxes. The next section outlined the profits you'd make down the road. If you were in the right tax bracket, this investment made you a ton of money as long as they didn't do something stupid like break even.

"Interesting reading?" I turned around and found myself staring at a young blonde woman. "I'm Terri. I work right over there for Ed Sullivan. Don't laugh, he's sensitive about his name. You're Campbell's temp, right?"

"Ted. Ted Duda."

"Let me show you where the coffee is." She wore a skintight dancer's top in lavender and a black wrap-around skirt of the same material. Her shoes were black, unusually bland, and had a modest heel. I learned later they were character shoes, favored by actresses because they were generic enough to cover many periods in history. Terri was an actress.

"You're with Carolyn's Crew, aren't you?" she asked as we walked.

"Yes."

"Me, too. Half the people here are temps. Business is booming. They can barely keep up." We got to a small, windowless room that contained a break table, a refrigerator, and a large coffee machine. "Well, here we are." She showed me how to make coffee if I needed to and encouraged me to take a cup. I did.

"Are you a theater person?" I could tell she was sizing me up, trying to figure out if I was straight. If I was a theater person, chances went down substantially.

"No, I'm not." I realized I'd failed to think through a cover story. I was going to have to come up with one on the fly.

"How did you find Carolyn's Crew, then?"

"I'm a friend of Bobby Martin."

"Oh." She was clearly disappointed. If I was a friend of Bobby Martin, then I must be gay. Apparently, she'd been hoping otherwise. "So, what are you into?"

Having borrowed Daniel's middle name, I went ahead and took more of his life. "I'm studying to be a librarian."

She gave me an odd look. "Okay. So, why aren't you working at a library?"

"Actually, I'm starting graduate school in the fall. So... I'm just trying to make some money until then." It was a bad cover story. Full of holes I'd have to fill in later—like for one, I was a little old for college. Fortunately, Campbell Wayne walked by the break room just then, and Terri ushered me back to his office.

In his late twenties, Campbell Wayne was an inch or two over six feet tall, nearly as tall as I am. He was elegantly thin, with long arms and legs that he arranged in such a way that he always seemed posed. Lithe is the kind of word you'd use to describe him. He looked like he could bend around corners. His hair was that kind of light brown that turns blond on top just from walking down the street, while remaining dark beneath. His eyes were brown, and his skin always seemed to be just recovering from a flush.

He wore a perfectly tailored, gray, three-piece, pinstriped suit with a pastel pink shirt and a navy blue tie. His shoes were worth more than my car.

Terri introduced us, and he said, "Welcome aboard, Ted." Then, without a word of instruction, dismissed me by saying he needed to make a call. When we got out to my cubicle, I turned and looked at Terri.

"He gets like that. Don't worry about it."

I took my jacket off and put it on the back of my chair, being careful not to let the gun in my pocket bang against anything. I looked around and tried to acquaint myself with my desk. It held a complicated phone, a large, book-sized calendar and an IBM Selectric with an opaque plastic cover. Fortunately, it was quiet that morning. There were only two calls, both from Julie Monroe, Campbell's fiancée. He took the calls quickly. The mail came around ten. I neatened up the stack and brought it in to him. He was reading the *Daily Herald* and didn't bother to look up.

Around eleven, he came out and gave me two invoices he wanted me to type check requests for. He showed me where to get the blank forms, then took me back to a file room where the carbons for the completed requests were filed and suggested I use an old check request as a template. If I had any problems, I should ask Terri. I didn't have any problems; the forms were straightforward enough. Both were to vendors for printing services rendered. About twenty minutes later I brought them into his office to be signed.

He scratched his signature on the bottom of both requests. "Make copies of each. This one," he pointed at the request with the lesser amount, "Kelly Graphics, can go interoffice to AP. Blanchard Designs needs to be signed by Ed Sullivan first."

Trying not to smirk at the mention of Ed Sullivan, I asked, "What's the difference between them?"

He gave me a look that made me wonder if asking questions was a breach of office etiquette. Finally, he said, "Blanchard Designs needs a second signature because it's over five thousand." Then he added, "Will there be anything else?"

I mumbled a "no, sorry" and left the room.

At lunch, I walked over to Water Tower Place. I thought I might be able to talk to Jeanine Anderson, but when I got to the seventh floor, I immediately saw that there was a line to get into The Gold Mine. A frazzled hostess, who was probably Jeanine, argued with a potential diner. She was pretty in an everyday way. Her skin was pink and fresh. A short woman, she was light on top and thick from the waist down. I figured she probably hated herself because she didn't look like a model. I also figured guys took advantage of that. She was so busy there was no way she'd be able to take the time to talk to me. I'd have to come back another day during my morning coffee break.

Taking the elevator back down to the first floor, I set myself up at the payphone I'd found on my previous trip. I took Lenny's bank statement out of my jacket pocket and called his bank. His mother had given me his birth date and her maiden name. As it turned out, this was enough to convince the woman in customer service I was the late Lenny Borlock. I told her about the suspicious charge and asked her what we should do.

She clicked her computer a few times and may have even shuffled some papers around. A few moments later she was back on the phone. "You called about this before, Mr. Borlock."

"Yes, that's right," I improvised.

"The deposit was made with one of the pre-printed slips that come with your checks. And the signature on the back of the check matches the signature card you gave us." Her tone suggested she was vaguely displeased.

"Are you sure it's my signature?"

"We're not handwriting experts, Mr. Borlock, but it does appear to be yours, yes. Are you sure you didn't make this deposit?"

"Who's the check from?" I asked, then hastily added, "I mean that might help me remember."

"LB Services." That didn't mean anything to me— other than L and B were Lenny's initials. "Would you like to take this any further?" she asked.

"Not right now, thanks." I said goodbye and hung up.

Lenny had already called them and set the investigation of the deposit in motion. That meant he didn't know where the deposit had come from. Someone with access to his checkbook had made the deposit, someone who'd been able to reasonably fake his signature. But why? Why give Lenny money? And why such an odd amount? Three thousand, five hundred, and sixty-four dollars? I folded up his bank statement and went back to work.

When I got back to the forty-second floor, a frightened secretary was running around telling everyone the president had been shot. Within minutes, half the company had tromped by my desk on their way to find a radio. The youngest people on the floor seemed unfazed. The older ones were thrown back to the sixties. Even the ones who didn't much like the Gipper couldn't help but think about Martin Luther King and the Kennedy brothers. Most everyone on the floor spent the rest of the afternoon standing in an office down the hall listening to a clock radio. Even Campbell went down for a while. I stayed at my desk.

Taking the opportunity, I slipped off my jacket and then looked around my workstation as thoroughly as I could. In the drawers, there was nothing but supplies. I knew that already. There were overhead shelves with flip-up doors. I peeked in there, but there was nothing but empty folders. I ran my fingers above the overheads, but only found dust.

I got down on my knees and crawled under the workstation. The two-drawer file cabinets were not attached to the desk surface and were moveable. I slid one out and peeked behind it. Nothing. After pushing it back, I crawled around to the other side of the workstation and was about to do the same with the other file drawer when a flash of white caught my eye. I looked up and saw an envelope taped to the underside of the desk.

Carefully, I peeled the tape back and pulled the envelope away from the wood. The envelope had already been opened, and I slipped out its contents. In a glance, I saw that it was a bill for a post office box. It was sent to Lenny, but the address was JTM, not his apartment. I was ready to get up and slip the envelope into one of the drawers, when I heard Campbell's voice behind me, "Lose something?"

Quickly, I slid the envelope under the two-drawer file cabinet and yanked a button off my shirt. I stood up. "I popped a button." With two fingers, I pulled open my shirt and showed him my navel.

He looked at the sliver of belly for a moment, raised his eyes to meet mine, and said, "I thought only fat people popped buttons."

"It's an old shirt."

# # #

The next few days were hectic. JTM V was launching in less than two months and the brochures weren't even begun. Half a dozen designers showed up for meetings with Campbell to show him possible ideas for the next brochure. Most of them seemed to be friends of his from when he was a student at The Art Institute. I had to keep all the appointments straight even though they kept moving around, conflicting with his social life and his workout routine. Plus, I had to make sure the conference room was booked for the larger meetings.

I found I didn't much like being a secretary; it was hours of boredom punctuated by brief periods of humiliation. The work was dull, and if I took even the smallest initiative, Campbell shut me down. Every day I reminded myself that next time I tried some kind of undercover work, I should pick something a little more interesting. Or maybe I should skip undercover work entirely.

To make matters worse, Campbell had put me at the disposal of his fiancée, Julie Monroe. They were planning a

Christmas wedding, and several times a day she called and issued commands in a way that made me think she was Cleopatra in a past life. Wednesday afternoon she read me a list of thirty guests to call who'd RSVP'd but neglected to check off chicken or fish. It took so long, I wondered if it wouldn't have been faster had she just called them herself.

Meanwhile, people on the floor were still talking about the president getting shot. It was pretty clear the old guy was going to be okay, so I didn't know what the fascination was. I overheard Terri talking with a secretary from accounts payable. Both seemed to think the president was dead and "they" were stalling to give them time to put in a look-alike. Whoever "they" were. One of the sales guys came by and made it clear he disagreed. The president was alive. The cover-up had to do with the fact that the Russians were behind the assassination attempt. "They" were hiding that fact to avoid nuclear war.

Even though things were busy, during lunch on Tuesday I managed to get under the two-drawer file cabinet and retrieve the invoice for the PO Box. Studying the invoice didn't tell me much more than I already knew. It didn't make sense that Lenny would rent a PO Box and then have the bill sent to the office. It was a renewal. That meant he'd rented the box six months ago, and since he was a temp, it made no sense to have the bill sent to a job he might not be at when it came due.

And it made even less sense to hide the invoice.

Wednesday was April Fools' Day. Right after the afternoon coffee break that I'd ended up working through, Campbell came out to my desk. He gave instructions on some calls he wanted me to make, one of which was to call around and see if I could find someone to soften the leather seats in his three year-old BMW—I half expected him to say, "Ha-ha, April Fools'" on that one. Unfortunately, he didn't.

"I know this is none of my business, but I heard the last guy killed himself," I said as casually as possible.

"Not the last guy, the guy before that."

"Oh. Do you know why he killed himself?"

"We didn't discuss it."

"There weren't any signs?"

He looked up at me. "I suppose. He came into work a few times high on something. You're not going to come to work high, are you?"

"No."

"Good. And you're not planning to kill yourself?"

"No."

"Then we'll get along fine."

I wanted to ask more questions, but knew I was pushing it. As casually as I could, I said, "He must not have been here very long."

"What do you mean by that?"

"I mean, if he'd been here a long time, you would have noticed more." And, though I didn't say it, might seem to care.

"He was here six months. But it's an office. People don't bring their dirty laundry here." The final bit was said almost as a warning. Then he turned and went back into his office. He'd managed not to tell me anything more than he'd told the police. But still, it was strange. When a person you knew killed themselves, it seemed normal to gossip about it, cathartic even. But Campbell seemed to discourage talk about it.

I still held onto the idea that Lenny had killed himself and was looking for the reason. Yes, there were things that made me suspicious: the money, the post office box, and, of course, the hostess who may have lied about what she saw the morning Lenny died. I did my best to work out explanations. The hostess may just have wanted the attention being a witness can bring. That was easy enough to explain. The money was harder. I might have considered blackmail if it wasn't such an odd amount.

Yeah, I was becoming increasingly suspicious that something else might be going on or there was at least more to Lenny's suicide than met the eye. By Thursday, I gave up the idea of suicide completely.

Around two o'clock that afternoon, the phone rang. "Campbell Wayne's office," I said, when I picked it up.

"Is he there?" A woman asked.

"Who's calling, please?"

"Jeanine Anderson." My skin went cold. Campbell knew her. I buzzed him and said there was a Ms. Anderson on the line. He took the call right away.

Campbell knew the one witness to Lenny's suicide. The one witness who couldn't have seen what she said she'd seen. That was it for me. Mrs. Borlock was right; Lenny hadn't killed himself. There were too many inconsistencies. Too many unexplained loose ends. But what had happened to Lenny?

# # #

That night I called Detective Harker and gave him enough information to get him interested. He suggested we meet for a drink at a bar on Sheffield. I'd heard of the bar before, Woody's; they served cheap drinks and catered mostly to the starving actors working in the nearby storefront theaters.

Woody's was about four blocks from where Daniel and I got bashed. On the way from my apartment, I walked by the spot—as I often did. It was a small, futile act of defiance. I refused to let those kids ruin the city for me. They'd taken enough from me.

I walked into the bar. It looked straight out of the fifties: red vinyl stools, booths along one wall, a jukebox filled with rockabilly. Harker got there about fifteen minutes after I did. He wore the same wrinkled tan suit I'd seen him in before and a bad case of five o'clock shadow. I guessed that his caseload was pretty heavy, and I wasn't helping things. After looking the place over, as though to make sure he didn't know anyone there, he walked over to me.

"You're not going to be too popular if we have to open this thing up again," he said when he sat down.

"I'm not too popular as it is." In general, I have to put up with a low level of police harassment—mostly from relatives. It hadn't been bad lately, but something like this was likely to kick it up again.

"Tell me again what you've got," he said after he ordered a scotch and water.

"In her statement, Jeanine Anderson said she could see Lenny hanging around the spot he jumped from while she was setting up at her station. If you stand right where she claims to have been, you can only see the elevator."

"What else?"

"Jeanine Anderson and Campbell Wayne have some kind of relationship."

"What kind?"

"I don't know. All I know is that she called him today."

"And the money?"

"There's a deposit to Lenny's account from a company called LB Services. The amount is weird. Three thousand, five hundred, and sixty-four dollars. He called customer service about it. It seems he wasn't expecting the deposit. And then there's the PO Box. I found a copy of an invoice for a PO Box taped to the bottom of Lenny's desk. Like he was hiding it. But there's nothing weird about it."

"Except why would a kid like Lenny need a PO Box?"

"Exactly," I replied.

Harker chewed it all over for a minute. "I'll poke around, ask a few questions, and then maybe reopen the whole thing. It's gonna be a few days, though." I nodded. "In the meantime, I want you out of there."

"Why? I'm getting good stuff."

"For one thing, it doesn't go down so well with a jury if a PI has to testify to most of the evidence. Nothing personal, but juries aren't all that fond of you guys. Plus it makes us cops look bad." He paused and looked me right in the eye. "For another thing, if this guy has killed a man, you could get hurt."

"He killed a kid who wrote poetry. I used to be a cop. It's not the same thing."

"I don't like it."

"It's not up to you."

He looked like he wanted to say more. A whole lot more. But he kept his mouth shut as we finished our drinks.

Outside the bar, we had an awkward moment saying goodbye. I couldn't tell exactly what was going on with Harker. He placed a hand on my shoulder and squeezed. I was suddenly hyper-aware of him standing close to me. I took a step back.

"I want you to be careful," he said. Before he walked away he handed me his card.

"You already gave me one of these."

"And now I'm giving you another. If you need me, I want you to be able to find me." The way he said it made me wonder exactly how many situations might qualify as *needing* him.

#

On Friday around noon, Julie Monroe showed up. She walked in like she owned the place, and being daughter to the M in JTM, she kind of did. She wore a tight black suit with a fur collar and sleeves that didn't make it all the way to her wrists. Her hair was dyed a flat black, and her lips were painted fire engine red. From the way she dressed, you could tell her favorite movie was anything starring Joan Crawford. The only thing that kept her from looking like a time tourist from the forties was the clump of hair over her left eye she'd had dyed fluorescent pink.

She stopped at my cubicle and gave me the kind of smile that says, "I don't like you, but I have to deal with you."

"You're Ted?"

"Yes."

"I'm Julie Monroe." She looked me up and down while I said it was nice to meet her. She didn't bother to say the same. "Can I speak to you? Privately?"

She'd said it quietly and sweetly, so as I followed her to a conference room I was sure she was going to ask me to help surprise Campbell with a party for his birthday or pick out a special gift for the wedding. When we got into the empty room, she shut the door.

"Campbell doesn't think I know about his little flirtations, but I do. So I just want to warn you...stay the fuck away from him." Her tone was hard and flinty. It crossed my mind that if I refused, she might pull a small Colt out of her purse and shoot me.

She didn't wait for an answer; instead, she threw her shoulders back and marched out of the room. I was in shock. I'd known there was a possibility that Lenny had had a crush on Campbell. Nothing about Campbell had suggested that the feelings might have been returned.

When I got back to my cubicle, Campbell was standing there with Julie—her right hand possessively draped over his shoulder.

"What's up with you two?" he asked.

"Nothing. Just wedding stuff," Julie lied.

They floated off into Campbell's office, but not before he asked me to make them a reservation at The Gold Mine. Campbell shut the door to his office.

I sat at my desk for a few minutes. I wondered if I was wrong about Campbell. Maybe he didn't kill Lenny. So far, I hadn't found a reason for him to do it, while his fiancée had just told me she had a strong motive. I wondered if Lenny had had a similar confrontation, and how far Julie might have gone if he'd ignored her.

Julie was tall for a woman, but I doubted she'd have the upper body strength to force even a small man over the railing at Water Tower Place. Still, she had more than enough money to pay someone. Maybe it wasn't about Campbell. Maybe I was following the wrong lead entirely.

I called the restaurant and a hostess answered. I took a chance and said, "Is this Jeanine?"

"Yes," she said skeptically.

"I thought so. I recognized your voice." I decided to do my best to imitate Bobby's chatty demeanor. "It's a nice voice by the way. Melodious."

"Who is this?"

"Campbell Wayne's secretary, Ted. Well, my friends call me Teddie. You called Campbell yesterday, didn't you? Or am I mixing you up with someone else? Oh, God, if I am, I'm sorry." My impersonation of Bobby wasn't especially good. I was a little stiff. But as long as she didn't know what I was doing, it passed.

"Oh. What can I do for you?"

"Campbell wants a reservation for two. He's bringing over his fiancée. Do you know her? I just got my first look at her. I'm not sure what to think."

Jeanine was silent for a moment. "So, it's two at one o'clock?"

"Oh gosh, he didn't say. Should I go ask him?"

"He always comes at one."

"Thanks. You really saved my butt." The whole company went to lunch at one. But she didn't have to know that. "Come on, you must have an opinion. Ice Queen or Sexy Tiger... I can't tell—"

"She's not his fiancée, she just thinks she is," Jeanine spat, and then hung up. That told me something. Their relationship was romantic, at least on Jeanine's end. Campbell seemed to have a way with the ladies...and, if his fiancée was right, the gentlemen, too.

After Campbell and Julie left to go to The Gold Mine, I took my little black address book out of my jacket, looked up Ross' number, and gave him a call. He picked up the phone, and from the groggy sound of his voice, I could tell I'd woken him up. I apologized and launched into the reason for my call, "Did you ask Earl the thing I wanted you to ask him?"

"Mmm-hmmm."

"Okay. What did he say?"

"The guy's a fake. Pretends to come from money, but nobody knows his family. He throws a lot of money around. Picks up tabs everywhere he goes. Hands out coke like it's candy."

"He's not dealing, is he?" That would explain where he was getting the money to throw around.

"No. Earl didn't say that, and I think he would have. People are noticing that this guy spends a lot more money than he's making. That's really all he said."

"Thanks, I appreciate it. Could you ask him to check out the fiancée, as well? There's something not right there."

"Sure, no problem."

He was about to hang up when I stopped him. "You know, I didn't say this the other night, but I hope you and Earl are really happy together."

"Thanks, Nick."

After my chat with Ross, I spent the rest of my lunch hour eating a sandwich I'd brought from home and poking around at the secretarial work I was supposed to be doing. It wasn't hard work, but it did get in the way of investigating Lenny's death. Campbell had been giving me check requests to type all week. I now had a stack of carbons that needed to be filed. When the clock hit two o'clock, I asked Terri if she'd watch my phones and headed into the file room.

The room was small, narrow, and lined with four-drawer file cabinets. There were two cabinets for Campbell's department, and the drawers that I needed were the top two of one of them. Each check request had two copies: one marigold and one green. The marigold copies were stapled to the original invoice and were to be filed by payment date. The green were to be filed by payee. While still at my desk, I'd put them in proper order so it wouldn't take me very long at all to collate them into the files.

The marigold copies were easy to file. For the most part, they slipped in behind the previous check requests. I did that, then went on to the green stack. I'd only filed a couple invoices when a thought hit me. Quickly, I flipped through the files to the L's. Right at the front was LB Services. I pulled out all the invoices for LB Services, nearly two dozen. I flipped through them. All told, they added up to about eighty thousand dollars. Each invoice had been sent within the last six months. The final invoice was for three thousand, five hundred, and sixty-four dollars.

All of the check requests were signed by Campbell Wayne—except they weren't. Or at least they didn't appear to be. I compared the signature on the LB check requests to a random request. The signatures looked similar, but were obviously different.

If it weren't for Lenny questioning the LB Services deposit to his account, I'd say he was embezzling from JTM. But Lenny hadn't been embezzling. It had been meant to look like he had, and that meant Campbell had to be behind it. I checked the LB invoice. The company's address was a PO Box. I couldn't remember the number from the invoice, but it was probably the PO Box that Lenny had rented. Or, rather, that Campbell had rented in his name.

Somewhere there had to be a holding account—probably also in Lenny's name. It was likely that Campbell had removed most of the money in cash. The only reason I could think to make the deposit to Lenny's account was that Campbell was trying to make it look like Lenny was the guilty party. Something he'd obviously been planning all along. But then Lenny got the invoice for the PO Box. He must have started trying to figure out what was going on. Then he'd noticed the deposit into his account. He began looking around, figuring things out, and figured out enough to end up dead.

Of course, this wasn't the real scam. This was just the scam to support the scam. Campbell had been throwing money around to convince Julie and her family he was the kind of guy—

A click behind me told me that someone else had entered the file room. I turned around to see Campbell standing near the closed door. He pressed in the button that locked it. I moved my glance from the door handle to his face. He smiled. My face may have flushed a bit. I definitely felt like I'd just been caught with my hand in the cookie jar. Campbell didn't say anything. I expected he'd ask what I was doing. Possibly grill me on why it was taking me so long.

Without taking his eyes off me, he reached down and unzipped his expensive slacks. He reached in and pulled out his dick. Even flaccid, it was impressively long and thick. Quickly, I went over my options. The other secretary, Terri, had picked up that I was gay. She'd probably spread it around, so it was likely Campbell expected me to jump on his dick lickety-split. If I didn't, he might be suspicious. On the other hand, since I'd just figured out he was a murderer, sex wasn't all that appealing—not that you'd have known by my dick, which was hardening in my pants.

"I think we should keep things professional," I said, and tried to move by him to get to the door.

He blocked me, reaching out and grabbing me by the cock. "This doesn't seem very professional to me."

Embarrassingly, I was harder than he was. I tried to think if there was an advantage to my having sex with him. Would I be able to find out more information if I did? Would he be more willing to share information? And is this what he'd done with Lenny? Did he try to control Lenny—

He had me out of my pants and was jerking me off with one hand while he jacked himself with the other. I stared him in the eye, barely able to breathe. His eyes were a warm brown; if I didn't know better, I'd say they were kind. They seemed to search mine, questioning. I tried not to give anything away.

Holding our dicks together, he squeezed them tight with one hand and jerked them as one. He leaned over, ready to kiss me. I twisted my head away from him, letting him know I didn't want to kiss him. He laughed.

I looked him straight in the eye, daring him to continue. He dropped to his knees and took me in his mouth. Placing a hand at the base of my cock, he licked his way around the head. He teased and nuzzled me. Slipped my dick into his mouth, sucked on it, then let it fall out with a popping sound.

He didn't seem all that experienced. He was tentative and kept things very shallow. Losing patience, I pushed his hand away and pumped my cock deep in his throat. He gagged a little, and I told him, "Just relax."

My hands in his hair, I moved his head back and forth on my prick. Looking down, I could see that his cock was hard and he was jerking it furiously. I closed my eyes and let my orgasm go in several thick bursts down his throat. I held his head down on my dick as my breathing returned to normal.

He moaned deep in his throat, and I looked down to see him coming over his fist. I pulled my cock out of his mouth and put it back into my pants. Campbell took a handkerchief out of his pocket and wiped off his fist. "Next time, you'll have to be a little friendlier. It'll be more fun."

#

Back at my desk, I collected my thoughts. I decided it was best not to over-analyze what had just happened in the file room. The important thing was the case. I had enough information to get Campbell on embezzlement. And that meant he had a motive to kill Lenny. What I didn't have was opportunity. Could I place Campbell in Water Tower Place at the time of Lenny's fall?

Campbell sat in his office, calmly going over some memos he'd gotten earlier. If I turned, I could look right at him. I didn't turn. In fact, I did my best not to look at him. I suppose I could have walked out of there right then. Mrs. Borlock was paying me to find out what had happened to her son, and I was pretty sure I had the answer. But I was still enough of a cop that I wasn't going to walk away without making sure Campbell paid for Lenny's murder.

I spent a few minutes straightening up my desk while I decided what to do. My time card was sitting out. Carolyn had explained the simple form to me. All I had to do was write down my hours, sign it, and then at the end of the week have Campbell sign it, too. Then I was to give him one of the two carbons for his records. It hit me that

that's where Campbell got Lenny's signature to forge. And the fact that he'd gone to The Art Institute made forgery a snap.

Campbell's secretaries kept an appointment book for him. I flipped back to the day of Lenny's death. According to the book, Campbell was in a meeting with Ed Sullivan from nine-thirty to ten-thirty, which covered the time of Lenny's death. I closed the book and walked around my cubicle to Terri's.

I lowered my voice. "Campbell's working on this big memo. He's trying to remember when he met with Ed last. His book says March fourth, but he thinks that meeting was canceled."

After giving me a look, she flipped open her book. "That meeting was canceled. But they met a week later. Campbell doesn't forget things like that."

I shrugged and lowered my voice, "He dictated the memo to me. I can't read my own writing."

"March fourth is the day Lenny killed himself."

"What was that like?"

"I don't know. Kind of normal, I guess. I didn't notice anything weird until Campbell came back from doing some wedding thing around ten-thirty and asked where Lenny was. I didn't even know he was gone."

"Ted!" Campbell called for me. I shrugged at Terri and left. It would be better if I could find a witness to Campbell's being at the mall next door. But it helped that he wouldn't be able to say he was sitting in his office.

It suddenly occurred to me that the person who could place Campbell at the mall was probably Jeanine. She was lying about what she saw. She could have seen Campbell there with Lenny—he might have even given her some story about trying to save Lenny. Clearly, she was involved with Campbell in some way. She'd want to help him keep his name out of the newspaper. That was the nice end of the spectrum. It was also true that she might have seen the whole thing and had no scruples about lying for the man she—

"I want you to sit in on the meetings this afternoon," he said when I walked into his office. "Take notes."

His demeanor was exactly what it had been before the incident in the file room. He had more design meetings that afternoon. The designers who'd been in before were bringing revised designs for Campbell to look at. I nodded and went back to my desk.

There wasn't a good reason for me to be in those meetings. I could only think that Campbell wanted to keep an eye on me. He didn't want me talking to Terri or anyone else. I wondered if he suspected me of anything. Part of me wanted to skip out of there and go next door to The Gold Mine, but then I remembered Jeanine didn't work on Fridays, so it didn't matter anyway.

The meetings were boring. I took enough notes to look like I had a reason to be there, but I didn't bother doing it well. The likelihood that I was coming next week was pretty thin. Not to mention, I doubted Campbell would be on the job.

The last meeting went past five o'clock. When we said goodbye to the designers, everyone else on the floor was gone. I began to gather my things to leave when Campbell said, "I want to buy you dinner."

"Oh, thanks. You don't need to do that."

"I know I don't need to. I want to."

"I sort of have plans." I did, sort of. I wanted to go home and call Detective Harker, tell him all about Campbell.

"Cancel them," he insisted.

I wondered what he'd say over dinner. Would he incriminate himself further? Would I be able to make the case airtight? Morbid curiosity took hold of me, and I agreed to go to dinner with him.

We took a cab up to New Town, and Campbell had the driver drop us off in front of Ann Sather's on Belmont near the El station. The restaurant was a trendy spot for breakfast, but for dinner not so much. It was brightly lit and served heavy, Swedish-style dinners, making it an odd choice for a romantic Friday night.

Campbell acted as if it were a great choice and ordered shepherd's pie with a side of sauerkraut. I had Swedish meatballs with a side of applesauce. They didn't serve alcohol, so Campbell ordered a coffee while I stuck to water.

"There's a project I want you to work on." I was surprised when he said it. I'd thought dinner was related to our adventure in the file room. He didn't wait for me to ask what project, he just continued, "Accounts Payable called me asking some questions about a vendor named LB Services. On Monday, I want you to pull whatever we have on them, invoices, check requests. I have a feeling something unpleasant has been going on."

"Unpleasant how?"

"I have to initial all invoices before they're paid. Then I sign the check request. But as far as I know, we don't deal with a company called LB Services."

"Why do you think I'll find anything, then?"

"I think Lenny, the poor kid who killed himself, may have been stealing from the company."

"I'll check the files on Monday." I was glad I came. It was nice to see the final part of his plan set in motion. Of course, he wouldn't want to discover the embezzlement himself. He'd want someone else to do it. When I got the information together, he'd likely ask me not to mention he'd suggested I look. He'd claim it would make me look better if I found it on my own, or some crap like that. The blow job he'd given me was to get me on his side. I figured he was planning a couple more to keep me there.

During the rest of the dinner, we talked about nothing important. He asked me questions about my personal life, and I made up a lot of lies. Fortunately, this was nearly over and I wouldn't have to remember them. I thought about asking about his fiancée, it did seem like the kind of thing you'd bring up after a guy sucks you off— but I was afraid I'd somehow tip him off if I did.

When the check came, he made a show of paying for dinner. I thanked him, and we went out to the street. It had begun to rain again, just a soft drizzle, but enough to be unpleasant. Belmont is a busy street. Cabs and station wagons, filled with suburbanites out for a Friday night's entertainment, sped by on the slick street.

Abruptly, Campbell said, "The El's right here. Let's take it to my place."

"I think I'm going to call it a night," I said. I would have pretended to be tired, but it was only around eight o'clock.

"Oh." He sounded disappointed, but didn't press me. "Well, are we going in the same direction?"

"I live a few blocks from here."

"Oh, that's right." It took me a moment to wonder why he knew where I lived. I was about to ask him how he knew, when he pushed me up against a building. I thought he was going to kiss me. Instinctively, I turned my face away, but that just opened up his real target. His hand dove into my breast pocket, and before I could stop him he pulled out my Sig Sauer.

"I think we should take El," he said.

Staring down the barrel of your own gun is always persuasive. I turned to the west and headed toward the station house.

"Why are you doing this?" I asked.

"You're not just any temp. For one thing, you find it necessary to bring a gun to work. For another, you told Terri you were a friend of Lenny's roommate even though you pretended not to know Lenny."

"Okay. So I knew Lenny and I'm nosy. That's not a reason to take a guy's gun and hold it on him."

"Isn't it? Nick?" He smiled. "I did a very thorough search of your jacket. In addition to this lovely accessory, I found your address book with your name and address on the first page. So, who exactly are you, Nick?"

"I'm a private investigator hired by Lenny's mother. Whatever you're planning, it's a bad idea."

He took a moment to digest what I'd just said. "No. Letting you walk away. That's a bad idea."

He pushed me through the thickly painted door of the El station. Inside was an ancient ticket booth with a turnstile in front of it. Next to that were a couple of modern, automated turnstiles. Most of the structure was wooden, having been replaced countless times since it was built at the turn of the century.

I was in trouble. Campbell liked pushing people, and he was taking me up to an elevated platform. It wasn't hard to figure out he was planning to push me in front of a train. Something I'd rather not experience.

He shoved me in front of him up to the ticket window. A middle-aged black woman in a CTA uniform gave me a bored look. I glanced back at Campbell. He was looking away, hoping the woman wouldn't be able to get a good look at his face. This gave me an opportunity, and I went for it.

I dug around in my pocket for change, and with the change I found the card that Detective Harker had given me. I slid the change and the card to the ticket taker. After a glance at Campbell, I tapped on the counter and, when the woman looked up at me, mouthed the word "Help." Then I walked through the turnstile.

Campbell threw some money into the window and was through. He shoved me up the stairs to the platform. I glanced back and saw the ticket taker watching through the dirty glass of the booth. A young couple had come through the door and dropped tokens into the automated turnstiles.

I could have fought Campbell every step of the way up the stairs. But my police training kicked in. I had an offender with a gun, and I needed to make sure he didn't hurt any innocent bystanders. If I fought too hard, someone might try to help me. I didn't want to be responsible for anyone else getting hurt.

When we got to the platform, a dozen people waited for the northbound train. We weren't far from the stairs when I dug my feet in and began to resist Campbell's efforts to lead me to the edge of the platform. Campbell didn't want to attract attention any more than I did. He didn't want any witnesses.

I'm sure he'd been hoping for a larger crowd. That would have given him more anonymity. In a smaller crowd, he couldn't afford to draw attention. That was my advantage. A train was coming, and people began moving forward. The sound of it grew as it came closer and closer to the station. Campbell tried again to move me forward, but I wouldn't budge. He poked the gun in my back and said, "Move."

"You're not going to shoot me," I told him. "Not with all these witnesses."

The train pulled into the station. People got on; people got off. Campbell kept me still until the train pulled out and the platform cleared. We were alone on our side, staring at the small group of people on the opposite platform. We were deadlocked. He knew if he waited for the next train there'd be a new crowd of witnesses. I could sense that he was nervous, unsure what to do next.

Unexpectedly, he yanked me sideways. Pushing and pulling, he led me over to the bridge people used to transfer to the opposite platform and the Ravenswood. It was a rickety-looking contraption that probably dated back to the beginning of the transit system. It went up ten steps, turned, and went up another seven. An open bridge crossed the tracks.

People on the opposite platform began to stare. What did we look like, I wondered? Did we look like a killer and his next victim? Or did we look like boyfriends who'd drunk too much at happy hour? I tripped, and Campbell dragged me up the first ten steps.

I didn't want there to be any kind of incident before the police got here. *If* they got here. I tried not to think about what would happen if the ticket taker hadn't called Harker. Of course, I knew that when we got to the center of the bridge, Campbell would try to push me off. I put up a fight at the landing between the two sets of steps. He was actually pretty strong. It was likely his workout routine was more intense than mine.

"You're not getting away with this," I told him. "A second secretary committing suicide? No one's going to believe that."

"They'll believe what I make them believe," he said arrogantly. "People always believe me."

I heard a train coming from the north. I turned to see how far away it was and lost my footing. Campbell was able to push me up the second set of steps to the bridge itself. I braced my feet so he couldn't get me to move any further, but he put a foot behind mine and pushed. I lost my balance and took a few steps back to keep from falling. We were very nearly over the southbound track.

The train got closer. Campbell was on me, one hand on my chest pushing, the other lifting my leg. I felt myself going over. I grabbed for the railing with my right hand. The sound of the train coming grew louder, forcing out all other sounds. Campbell gave me a final push and I was over the railing. I had a good grip on the railing, but the force of my body swinging over the railing made it nearly impossible to hold on. I looked down, and the train was coming into the station beneath me. I let go.

I landed on top of the moving train. I wasn't able to get my footing on the smooth metal of the roof. I slid off, falling onto the wooden strip between the tracks. When I landed, my right leg hit at a bad angle and a sharp pain ripped through me like an electrical current. A second later I lay on the strip, the wheels of the train still moving inches from my face.

# # #

Later, I heard that Detective Harker and several patrol officers had arrived in time to see Campbell push me off the bridge. They arrested him, then stopped the trains until they could get me off the track.

My leg turned out to be fractured just below the knee, which meant they had to stabilize my knee, so I ended up with a cast from my ankle to the middle of my thigh. I spent a lot of the first week hanging around my bedroom until I got a handle on the crutches. Mrs. Borlock insisted on helping me out and came by every day. She even tacked a little bonus onto her check. I would have objected to both, but the truth was I needed the help. Bobby and Freddie came by and brought some Birds of Paradise they'd bought at a florist on Broadway.

That Tuesday, I finally got around to reading Lenny's poetry. It wasn't as bad as Freddie had suggested. It wasn't good, but I'd expected it to be the literary equivalent of

Freddie's penis paintings, and it was better than that. I guess I'd call them everyday poems. They talked about the things Lenny did with his friends and his mother. They showed Lenny to be what people thought him to be, a happy guy. But more than that, he knew it. He appreciated his life, his friends, even his mother—he wrote a couple sticky-sweet poems about her that choked me up a little.

After I read the poems, I called her into my bedroom and told her, "I think you should read these. There's a little bit of sex stuff in some of them, but I think you can handle it." She took the composition notebooks and clutched them the way she had her photo album the first day she came to my office. "I will, eventually." Knowing what had happened to her son hadn't relieved her pain as much as she'd hoped, but I think it made it survivable. I don't think she'd been able to begin grieving until she knew for sure he hadn't killed himself. Now that she knew, the grieving began.

The doorbell rang, and Mrs. Borlock went to answer it for me. A few moments later, she came back with Detective Harker. He wore the same tan suit he'd worn every time I saw him, and it still looked slept in. They stood by my bed, and we chatted for a few moments, then Mrs. Borlock said she needed to leave. I was surprised, since I expected Harker would have information about what was happening with Campbell Wayne, but the look on her face said she'd had enough for the day. I promised to bring her up to date the next time I saw her.

When she was gone, Harker jumped into the facts of the case without being asked.

"When we searched Wayne's apartment, we found a set of fake IDs with Lenny's name and Wayne's picture. We're not sure yet where he got them."

"He probably did them himself. He went to The Art Institute."

Harker nodded agreement. "We've interviewed Jeanine Anderson three times. She's sticking to her story. The last time she came in, she came in with an attorney from the same firm Campbell Wayne's using."

"What's going on with Campbell?"

"He's not saying much. Except that he doesn't know anything about the embezzlement or Lenny's death. He claims the two of you were having an affair and what happened at the El was just a lover's spat gone bad."

"I guess I shouldn't be surprised."

"Did you have sex with him?"

"No. He came on to me, but I turned him down," I lied. It was better if Harker didn't know. And I wasn't especially proud of what had happened in the file room.

"You think he's gay?" he asked me.

"Guys like that, I think it's more about manipulation than sex."

Harker thought about that for a moment. "The Monroes are standing by him. Paying for his lawyers."

"He'll go to prison, though?"

"Yes. He'll go to prison."

That seemed to finish our business, and an awkward silence fell.

"Thanks," I said.

"For what?" he asked.

"You kept forcing your card on me. Turned out to be a good idea."

"I told you to get out of that office. That was a better idea."

Abruptly, he sat on the bed and put a hand on my left thigh. I was surprised and not surprised. He looked at me, a question in his light blue eyes. I sat up further and kissed him. For such a gruff guy, his lips were surprisingly soft. I pulled him back onto the pillows with me, and we kissed for a long time.

Eventually, he sat back and opened the front of my pajamas. After playing with the hair on my chest, he leaned over and began to lick my nipples, one at a time. Quickly, they turned to hard little nubs. He rested his head on my chest and wrapped his arms around me as best he could. "I'm glad you're okay," he whispered.

I pushed him away and undid his tie, then quickly unbuttoned his shirt. I pushed his shirt and his jacket off at the same time. They landed somewhere on the floor.

His chest was sinewy and covered in a thin layer of blond hair. He leaned away from me, running his hand down my belly and opening my pajama bottoms. Reaching in, he pulled out my hard cock. Before he began sucking me, he ran his tongue the length of my dick, ending by spinning it round and round the tip.

Harker might be a bit socially awkward, but he knew his way around a man. While he sucked me off, he played with my balls. Caressing them, pulling them gently, rubbing them between his fingers. With his other hand, he opened his pants and began to jack himself off. I caught a glimpse of his prick. It looked to be like the rest of him, short and a bit thick, veins standing out proudly.

He stood up and got rid of his shoes and his pants. When he got back onto the bed, he straddled me. Reaching behind me, he took me in hand and lined my dick up with his asshole.

"Do you have anything? I'm not going to be able to do this with just spit."

I reached over to the nightstand and opened the drawer, pulling out a small jar of Vaseline. I handed it to Harker, who spread it liberally over both of us.

Slowly, he eased himself down onto me. When he got me all the way inside of him, he asked, "Is this okay?"

"It's fine. It's more than fine."

He began to move up and down on my dick. Carefully at first, then more rapidly as he loosened up. I took his cock in hand and jacked him off as he bounced up and down on me. He was careful not to lean back and put pressure on my legs—but all the movement did cause a little ache in my leg. I didn't say anything, though. There wasn't a chance in hell I was going to let him stop.

Leaning over, he kissed me again and again, while still managing to pump me with his ass. His breath was short, and his mouth hung open in concentration, but he never took his eyes off mine.

I sensed he was close, so I jacked him off faster while making sure each stroke took in the head of his dick. His thighs quivered and his belly shook and then he was coming all over me.

He paused for a moment, then began again. "Come inside me," he said. I squeezed my eyes together and concentrated. For a moment, I thought I might not be able to do it, but then I was coming hard and fast. I let out a deep growl.

Harker fell forward onto my chest. His body was warm and a little damp. As I ran my fingers through his stubbly blond hair, he looked up at me and said, "Hey, you."

I couldn't help but feel my life was changing, shifting, turning into something it hadn't been for a very long time. And strangely, that was all right with me. I smiled at Harker and said, "Hey."

ALSO BY MARSHALL THORNTON

Desert Run

Full Release

The Perils of Praline, or the Amorous Adventures of a Southern Gentleman in Hollywood

The Ghost Slept Over

My Favorite Uncle

IN THE BOYSTOWN MYSTERIES SERIES

Boystown: Three Nick Nowak Mysteries

Boystown 2: Three More Nick Nowak Mysteries

Boystown 3: Two Nick Nowak Novellas

Boystown 4: A Time For Secrets

Boystown 5: Murder Book

Boystown 6: From The Ashes

Boystown 7: Bloodlines

Marshall Thornton is a novelist, playwright and screenwriter living in Long Beach, California. He is best known for the *Boystown* detective series, which has been short-listed in the Rainbow Awards three times and has twice been a finalist for the Lambda Book Award - Gay Mystery. Other novels include the erotic comedy *The Perils of Praline, or the Amorous Adventures of a Southern Gentleman in Hollywood*; *Full Release*; *The Ghost Slept Over* and *My Favorite Uncle*. Marshall has an MFA in screenwriting from UCLA, where he received the Carl David Memorial Fellowship and was recognized in the Samuel Goldwyn Writing awards. He has also had plays produced in Chicago and LA, and stories published in *The James White Review* and *Frontier Magazine*.

41540273R00144

Made in the USA
Middletown, DE
19 March 2017